MALACHI WHITAKER

The Crystal Fountain
and other stories

Introduction by Joan Hart

**PALADIN
GRAFTON BOOKS**

A Division of the Collins Publishing Group

LONDON GLASGOW
TORONTO SYDNEY AUCKLAND

Paladin
Grafton Books
A Division of the Collins Publishing Group
8 Grafton Street, London W1X 3LA

Published by Paladin Books
in association with Carcanet 1986

This selection first published in Great Britain by
Carcanet Press Ltd 1984

ISBN 0-586-08576-9

Printed and bound in Great Britain by
Collins, Glasgow

Set in Baskerville

Contents

Introduction

Malachi Whitaker's last book — a kind of autobiography called *And so did I* — was published early in 1939. Her press-cuttings book contains twenty-six enthusiastic reviews. This year I have been unable to find copies of any of her publications. The four volumes of short stories on which her reputation — if it still existed — would rest, were published by Jonathan Cape in the late twenties and through the thirties. In the forties a selection appeared, and a few short stories and occasional pieces were printed in *The Listener* and *John o'London's Weekly*. Then she announced to her family that she had written herself out. That was that. Well, almost. When she died, aged eighty, she left a few unpublished stories and some autobiographical pieces.

Certainly she had written a lot. At twenty, apparently, a fifty-thousand word autobiography! A novel in manuscript fell over-board from a cross-channel boat. There were years and years of tearing up; years and years during which she taught herself to write. Certainly it does not appear that anyone taught her: she just read, and then wrote. 'A born writer,' wrote Vita Sackville-West, reviewing her first published stories.

Marjorie Olive Taylor, the eighth in a bookbinder's family of eleven children, was born in Bradford in 1895. Her father's occupation gave her the opportunity to read the books that were lying around. Leaving school early, she worked for her father until, in 1917 she married Leonard Whitaker. As a writer she adopted the name Malachi, chosen from the Bible. She became Malachi, even to her friends.

Perhaps her juvenile autobiography, and all the years of tearing up, taught her how to write stories. Probably the writing of short stories helped her to find the extraordinary form — apparently quite random, but in fact amazingly controlled — of *And so did I*.

The prevailing tone of her writing — sad, salted with a sometimes violent humour — seems to reflect her native Yorkshire landscape: bleak, open, lit with pale sunshine.

I first became aware of her through her *Selected Stories*, published in 1946. Seeking something that might be acceptable as a 'Morning Story' for the BBC radio programme, I found — and I subsequently broadcast — 'Blackberry Day'. I was delighted to discover among her papers the contract for payment of £16 2*s*. I wonder how she spent the unexpected cheque. On something enjoyable, I'm quite sure. Her capacity for enjoyment was considerable.

But let her speak for herself. Here, as a preface to my selection from her stories, is her account of how the first one came to be published.

December 1983   JOAN HART

Beginnings

WHEN I saw downs for the first time they were familiar to me because of a cricket field I frequented at the age of four. This was only a small field. The pitch was in a hollow, and a grassy bank rolled gently up from it, to be crowned at the summit by a couple of eastward-bowing sycamore trees.

It was under one of these trees that I composed my first poem, ran home intoxicated across the cricket pitch, through a game in progress, stammered it breathlessly to my father, was given sixpence, and spent it, all within an hour. And almost thirty years later the same thing repeated itself in a more dignified fashion, with an editor in place of a father.

I live now within a few yards of that cricket field. The trees are cut down. A road runs through part of it, but I can still see it in its young-century beauty, feel the early summer warmth, know again the glory of the sun and the daisy that provoked the poem; because at that very moment (I could already read and write, being the eighth of a family of eleven) I became aware that I was in a marvellous place, that I was alive, and that I must say so.

My second poem was not so good. What I really wanted was another sixpence. I repeated my poem, which had given me a lot of trouble, but my father merely said, 'You're too late, lass. Shakespeare said this first, and much better,' and kept his hand in his pocket. So I went and pulled out a loose tooth — we got a penny for things like that — and thought a lot.

Afterwards, when I wrote anything, I would look at it for a long time, grow certain that somebody else had done it better, and tear it up. Anyhow, reading was so much pleasanter. I learned how to be deliberately naughty (I got noise of the ear-splitting kind into a fine art) so that I could be sent to bed where I could read in ecstasy, alone, and not have to look after one or more of my three little brothers.

Luckily for me my father was a bookbinder, so there were always plenty of books. Sometimes people would leave books at his place to bind, and forget to return them. They were put in an attic, and so was I. It is hard to remember the names of all of them. There was *David Copperfield* — though for many years I never got beyond page forty of him — *Wuthering Heights*, volume after volume of the *Family Herald Supplement*, *Tom Jones*, *Peregrine Pickle*, bound copies of *Tit-bits*, *All the Year Round*, and *To-day*, *Les Misérables* (how I ploughed through that one), *Andersen's Fairy Tales*, *Vanity Fair*, and an old Bible.

The ones I could not read were *Don Quixote* and *Jessica's First Prayer*. There was a Child's Bible which I tried, but did not find suitable after the real one. I would look for words like hell and devil in the real Bible, and simply go on reading, because I liked the rolling sound of the sentences. At my first school I got every Scripture prize going. There was also a book called *Little Meg's Children*, which delighted me at an early age. In that, or another very much like it, there were the words 'Perseverance, paint, and glue, Eighteen hundred and eighty-two.' I thought it a better poem than any of mine. And I was right.

At my second school I was a nasty child. I hated it so much, and was so miserable that I was forced to make a world of my own to get along at all. There was a three-mile walk to it, and that I enjoyed, summer and winter. There was so much to see, so much to do and think about. One of my favourite pursuits was following streams. If they went underground, so did I. But all I got was cold and dirty; I got torn clothes and smackings, too; and atmosphere.

There were no prizes, and no good marks of any kind for me at this school. I did my worst work at examinations, not from nervousness, but from contempt. And the whole of the time I was steadily writing and burning everything I wrote. Only once did I betray myself. We were told to write a story, and mine was read in front of the class. Feeble as it was, it was apparently the best of the lot. I was in an agony of shame. I remember telling the other girls that I had copied it out of a book. Somebody told the form-mistress, and she kept me behind and asked me why I was such a liar. I don't know what I said. All I wanted to do was get away.

About that time I read a story about a child who formed his letters so crookedly that one night they came out of the book, dragging themselves lamely in front of him, wanting to be made straight. That is what my own sentences still do. For a long time after my first book was published I used to wake in the night while badly expressed and broken paragraphs crept in chains of horror before my eyes. But I am trying to learn tolerance.

The war came then. Still determined to be a poet, I made up a set of windy martial verses, and sold them to a Christmas-card firm for seven shillings and sixpence. At the same time I was working twelve hours a day for from ten to twelve shillings a week. I use that as my excuse. Printed for some reason in mauve ink, these verses had the look of weak cocoa.

At the age of twenty I wrote my autobiography in fifty thousand words. I still have it. It amazes me by its arrogance. All I was not I put in that autobiography. Then I got married and went to live in France. And there I wrote a business novel, which, fortunately, fell overboard from a Channel steamer. I caught a quick view of these sheets of thick paper untidily strewing the sea, not realizing for some time that they were my novel.

Then for six or seven years I wrote nothing. But that did not stop my habit of thinking. My husband and I had a small house built on the top of a hill in Yorkshire, where there was a forty-mile view from the windows. I hadn't very much to do, and I used to look out of the windows a lot at the clouds, and wish that I had half-a-dozen children. It was no use wishing. I hadn't. I swopped an old gramophone for a typewriter — it was, I remember, a Salter Standard — the letters of which were both broken and invisible. It was a heavy thing, but I lugged it around with me, and learned to type on it.

One day in 1926 or '27, I am not sure of the year, I suddenly wrote a story straight through from beginning to end. I was absolutely amazed. I called it 'Sultan Jekker'. It was the first story I had written for a dozen years. At the age of fifteen I had written imitation Jack London, imitation Bret Harte, imitation anybody-who-took-my-fancy stories, and had them in an amateur magazine that used to be sent to my father's place to bind. But 'Sultan Jekker' was not an imitation. It was mine. I wrote it straight on to the Salter typewriter, not stopping to look at the words, which I couldn't have seen anyway.

Well, my first story was written. I showed it to my husband, and he was surprised too. We wondered what to do with it. We had not seen any of the same sort in popular magazines. But I found a different kind of magazine in the public library. It was called the *Adelphi*. I admired every contributor to this paper. There was a man called D. H. Lawrence, who had written two books that I had read — *Sons and Lovers*, and *Aaron's Rod*. I knew that he knew what he was talking about. He was the best contributor of all, I thought. And I thought, 'Very well, then. Go where the best is, or nowhere at all.'

All the same, I kept that story for a long time. I took it with me on a visit to London meaning to drop it in the letter-box of the *Adelphi*, which was then in Cursitor Street, Chancery Lane. I prowled about Chancery Lane every day for a week, never getting up enough courage to put it in the letter-box. I took it back home with me.

Then one day I put the story into a clean envelope, enclosed a stamped envelope for return — nothing else, not a single word of writing — addressed it very simply to the editor of the *Adelphi*, and posted it. There was an uphill walk of a mile from the post-box. I went back up the hill feeling as if I had committed a kind of crime. My husband tried to console me. 'They can't do anything worse than send it back.'

On the last day of March 1927 I got a letter. At that time I had very few correspondents, and a letter was an event. But this was in my own handwriting; I knew what it was, and did not want to open it. Of course I did open it eventually, and of course it contained my MS. There was also a note from John Middleton Murry, in his own handwriting. 'Dear Sir,' it ran, 'this is a *good* story. Unfortunately, in all human probability the *Adelphi* will be coming to an end after two more numbers, and I am therefore unable to accept it. If, however, you still find the *Adelphi* being published after June next, send your story to me again.'

I believe I could have walked straight off the cliff at the end of the garden, across to the moor top at the other side of the valley without going anywhere near the ground. Such was the effect of these words on me.

I waited to see if the *Adelphi* came out in September. But all the meantime I was writing away like one possessed. I wrote story after story in a trance. Very often they were badly worded. I was unable to get them right. Many of the stories in my first book I rewrote from ten to fifteen times. 'Frost in April' I typed out eighteen times. Quite boldly I sent a tale to a weekly called *Outlook*. It was taken and printed, and paid for, too, but I hardly noticed it, so hungrily was I waiting for the *Adelphi* to reappear.

In the September it did come out again, and within eighteen months at least five of my stories had appeared in the *Adelphi* — there and nowhere else. I don't believe I sent them anywhere else. I had no other desire than to be with this rich company of writers.

At that time Mr John W. Coulter was assistant editor. He was the first writing man I had ever met, and I thought he was half a god. I went with my husband to that office in Cursitor Street, and Mr Coulter thought that my husband was the writer, and talked to him all the time. We were on our way to Spain, and had our luggage with us. My husband is, above all, a business man, and knows more about the structure of cloth than about books. He was getting in a literary fog, saying yes and no in the wrong places, when I jumped up and said miserably, 'Look here, I wrote those stories.' I can still see Mr Coulter, looking like a schoolmaster behind a desk, with the two of us sitting in front of him like a couple of Will Hay's scholars.

On our return, Mr Murry wrote to say that if I had enough stories for a volume he would do his best, though he could not promise anything, to help me place them with some publisher.

There it was. I didn't have to ask anybody for a thing. It just happened.

One day in March 1929 I went up to meet Mr Murry himself. There was to be a luncheon at some restaurant, and I was asked to go. I was much too frightened to go. I was not used to eating in front of strangers, and did not want to choke. So I went merely to have coffee.

The place was up some stairs. There seemed to be a lot of people, but I only remember Mr Murry, Mr Coulter, Sir Richard Rees, and Dr James Young. I asked the latter if he was *the* Dr Jung, and he said no, a little coldly. My hands trembled so much that I could not lift my coffee-cup. Somebody — I believe it was Dr Young — made me take some wine, and I had alternate drinks of coffee and wine until I came round. They have told me since that they were all much more scared than I was, and I can believe it now.

When I had been there a few minutes I handed my bundle of

MSS to Mr Murry, saying briefly, 'I've brought these'. He had a case, and I had not. He put them in this case, oh so casually, and I hoped he would look after them, as I had not a whole copy of any story; but I am sure that, if he had lost them, I should have been able to write them all again by heart.

However, he kept them most carefully, and sent them to Mr Jonathan Cape. At his place they were read by Mr Edward Garnett, who wrote and told me that he, too, liked them. The next thing that happened to me was the signing of an agreement, and, a month or two after that, the arrival of some proofs. By now I was getting used to amazing things. On 14 October 1929 out came my first volume of stories, *Frost in April*. And then, for weeks, nothing else happened.

My first reviewer was Humbert Wolfe. He was taking Gerald Gould's page in the *Sunday Observer*, while Mr Gould was on holiday. Mr Wolfe was not sure. He sniffed gingerly round my stories. I do not remember his exact words, but he said of one of them that it was 'like a piece of fog cut out and preserved'. I was genuinely pleased with such unique criticism.

Then the late Mr Arnold Bennett gave me half a column in the *Evening Standard*, and for a week or two my name seemed to be in every paper I picked up. I was surprised to discover that I was a printed genius. There was only one dissentient voice. Somebody in the north of Ireland sneered at 'this boy's lemonade masquerading as man's wine'. Nearly everybody called me 'he' because of my biblical name.

Now there are four volumes with my name on the cover. If Mr Murry had not troubled to write to me about that first story, I should have gone on writing, because I could not have helped it. I might have returned to my childish habit of burning everything. Then there might have been a little less work for printers, binders, booksellers; a little less wearying on eyesight, and tongue, and brain. But none of us would have been any wiser, or any more ignorant, than we are now.

MALACHI WHITAKER
And so did I (1939)

Sultan Jekker

A FAT man, with loose, light-pink cheeks, was sitting on the side of a flat truck, eating his lunch. He had a torn gabardine raincoat on, and a cap so shrunken by rain that it made his face look enormous. His legs, which were short, did not reach the ground as he sat, and his feet hung inertly, toes pointing inwards. He faced the blank wall of a newly-stuccoed tram-shed, and ate slowly and with a vague sadness from some thick slices of white bread wrapped in newspaper.

He was not alone, there being four or five other men also on the truck, seated around it facing east, north, and west. They discussed starting-prices as they ate, and interlaced their exchange of news with loud and careless oaths. They did not trouble to lower their voices if a woman passed, which was not infrequently; and none of the corporation employees, hurrying in and out of the tram-shed like preoccupied ants, interfered with, or spoke to them. They were navvies, and had come out into the sunlight to eat.

Suddenly the fat man, whose name was Clarence Waterman, gave a loud shout, and said in a surprised, angry voice, 'The bitches! They said they would put some meat in.' He had just discovered that he was eating only bread, but his companions took no notice of him. It often happened this way. The big man lived with two women, who were for ever quarrelling and fighting over him, and sometimes they forgot altogether, in the bitterness of their early morning disputes, to put up any lunch at all for him. He swore he would beat them on his return home, but nearly always he forgot. His companions, who for some reason of their own called him 'Jekker', were proud of him, as they were all married, and thought of him and his two women with envy.

However, he was not to be envied. These women had come strangely into his life, and had as strangely stayed there, without his consent. They were violently jealous and frequently injured each other, their faces rarely remaining for a week free from marks of intense conflict. Before their coming, he had had peace. He had lived alone in an isolated cottage for fifteen years of his adult life, and at the age of thirty-five, within a fortnight, these two women, strangers, were living in the utmost intimacy with him and each other.

Phoebe, the elder, was a raddled blonde of about forty, with stout, flat feet, on which she wore men's boots, but no stockings. She sold lavender, also peppermint-cordial, which she made herself with essence and questionable water from the well behind the cottage. When these were out of season she hawked bootlaces. She had an impudent and ingratiating manner, and a certain hard stare with which to terrorize timid housewives. She was without a moral standard and had few womanly virtues. The first time she called at Jekker's cottage with her lavender and her cordial, she opened the door after repeated knockings to find the man seated on the hearth with a red shawl twisted around his head, groaning with toothache. Before he could stop her, she had pulled the aching tooth with one turn of her large brown finger and thumb. Later in the evening, she took him down to the inn, and stayed with him until he drank himself insensible. Then she alternately pushed and carried him home, picking him up as he fell. Once arrived, she pulled off his boots and drove him before her into the bedroom. He accepted her without surprise, as a fortnight later he accepted Caroline.

It was really Phoebe who invited Caroline to live with them. They met her at the Vine Leaf, the squalid house they patronized. She picked rags 'on piece', and drank to forget her husband, who, through miscalculation, would have to spend the next three years in gaol. She had reached the maudlin stage, and quiet tears were running endlessly down her cheeks when the inn-frequenters trooped out, disturbing the starry night, rapt with autumn silence. Phoebe, big with beer-engendered kindliness, was comforting her, saying, 'Don't cry, lass, there's many a better man, many a better man —'. The usually cautious Phoebe had had too much to drink, and was finding the way with difficulty. Jekker lingered, but she did not care, as she knew he had left the door-key under a stone.

Somehow she reached the cottage with Caroline, Jekker following. The long walk up the hill, the cart-ruts frozen hard and the tufted grass already white with rime, the complacent crow of an awakened rooster, they did not hear, see, or feel. All they wanted was further oblivion. Phoebe said that Caroline could sleep on the big horsehair couch in the kitchen before the fire. Jekker, stumbling in, lit the smelly paraffin lamp without accident, began to poke the fire which had been made up ready for their return, forgot, let the poker fall from his hand, and sprawled across a wooden chair, snoring a little in drunken stupor. Phoebe, on the horsehair couch destined for the rag-woman, was already fast asleep, her long, unlovely mauve-coloured lips hanging apart, and wisps of her light hair moving with each breath.

Caroline, slightly over thirty, dark, red-faced, in a stained, greeny-black dress, passed the back of her hand over her smeared face, and broke again into low sobbing. The noise awoke Jekker, who stared at her bemused, and then said in a beseeching voice, 'Now, Ca'line, now, Ca'line'. He had opened his small, dull eyes to their full extent, and his mouth looked like a red-plush button in the middle of his great face. The woman did not appear to find anything humorous about him, for she returned his stare long minutes, the tears lying unheeded on her red cheeks, and no others appearing to take their place. It was Phoebe alone who spent the night on the horsehair couch.

In the morning, the rage of the older woman was dreadful to see. The first of the endless fights took place, then tears of exhaustion, then a surly reconciliation. The man watched with apathetic looks. It was not his affair. They should fight it out, and let the best woman win.

It was not long before everything settled into routine. At first, the women stayed in the house the day long, not daring to go out, in fear of being locked out, but after furtive essays, expeditions to the yard and the well, they began to trust each other a little. Each wanted a home, a man. They also wanted food and drink, and as early on Jekker would not give them any money, they had to go out and earn some. The lavender-woman had no set times for working, and this would sometimes exasperate Caroline, who laboured for fixed hours, though on piece-work.

They passed the long winter evenings, when they did not drink, in making a rug of cloth pieces, which Caroline stole and brought home under her skirt. They had nothing to say, so they did not talk. The orange light from the lamp illumined the low-ceiled room with its two heavy beams. A square table, covered with brown linoleum, stood in the middle of the room. The couch, two or three wooden chairs, and a small, painted, wooden dresser was the extent of the furniture. There was nothing on the walls but a grocer's almanac of twenty years ago, going yellow and turning inwards in spite of the four rusty tacks which held it in place.

Phoebe had a secret passion for cosmetics, and would spend her spare pence on beautifiers, which gave her a grim and ugly look. She only used them when she wished to appear seductive before her unresponsive lord. Sometimes during the evening Phoebe would steal upstairs and come down after a while with rouge and powder on her hard, lined, impudent face, her hair grotesquely frizzled, and even crimson smears on her light-coloured lips. As soon as she opened the doorway at the bottom of the stairs, Caroline would break into ribald sneers. 'Come in, you beauty, you!' she would shout, along with other remarks, but Phoebe would not take the slightest notice of her, beyond a whispered 'Get out,' which command, curiously enough, the younger woman sooner or later always obeyed. Phoebe felt that, by right of priority, she ought occasionally to have the man to herself. Caroline did not care, as she was only existing until her own man came out of prison, yet often she stole the helpless prey successfully from out of the very hands of the older woman.

Jekker began to hate Phoebe, with her light-blue eyes, pulled down at the corners, and her flabby, creased cheeks, daubed clumsily with rank powder, with her attempts at coquetry, which the stolid, animal-like man did not understand. He preferred the buoyant Caroline, and began to follow her with his round, flat eyes, and to look to her for help, and to keep her in with appealing motions of his heavy arms when she would prepare to go out and leave him alone with Phoebe.

He wished that Phoebe would go, but he knew that she would not, and he had not the wit to devise a means of making her leave. Sometimes he locked the door on her, and kept her out all night, but she was always waiting in the yard, shouting and screaming from early dawn, and clawing for Caroline's face as soon as the younger woman came out, yawning, and twisting her straggling black hair with exaggerated nonchalance. He never locked Caroline out.

Over two years passed in strange companionship. As if they had been one real wife, he put money down each week on the brown-covered table, and let them buy food for him. At first, each had eaten separately, but they found it cheaper to share. So now he sat on the truck, and grumbled because his women had forgotten to put the meat he had paid for between his slices of bread.

His bread finished, and the last of the cold tea drunk from the dark-blue enamel can, he jumped down and stood morosely looking over the green landscape. A thin film spread over the face of the sun, and a whipping shower stung his face and made his cheeks quiver. The sky filled with low clouds and heavier, steadier rain began to fall. The navvies looked around. Perhaps they would be rained off, but they had already put a morning's work in, so they did not mind. After being dismissed, they tramped off sturdily, in twos or alone.

Jekker stumped along by himself. His legs were slightly bowed, as if bent by the massive body above him. He had buttoned his raincoat high, and walked with lowered head fronting the rain, the blue tea-can creaking in his right hand, thinking about Caroline, whom he liked, and Phoebe, whom he didn't like. An idea had come into his head that if he were to lock Phoebe out every night, say for a month, she would surely begin to realize that she was not wanted. He might try. Meanwhile, he climbed the hill to his home.

Phoebe was in the kitchen when he arrived, humming to herself and smiling in a secret way. She made him some tea, which he did not want, so he pushed the mug away and sat staring into the newly-lit fire. Then he pulled a plug of tobacco from his pocket, cut off some small pieces, rubbed them between his hands, and finally lit his pipe with a smouldering coal.

'Rained off?' casually enquired Phoebe, after an hour's silence.

He did not think it worth while to reply, in view of the rain which was now beating forcefully against the small window. Phoebe was engaged in washing his shirt and socks, a job which usually fell to Caroline.

Evening drew in earlier because of the rain. Still Phoebe moved about, the secret smile widening her wide mouth. She prepared the evening meal, for two.

'Where's Ca'line?' asked the man, breaking his afternoon's silence.

'How should I know?' parried Phoebe, but there was a laugh, a sound of triumph in her rough voice, which penetrated even the dull brain of Jekker, and made him look at her with eyes towards the surface of which some faint expression struggled.

They ate and drank noisily. After the meal, Phoebe cleared away and put the things into a cupboard. Then she turned the drying shirt and socks and things of her own that were airing near the fire. The evening wore away, ticked towards night by the tin alarm clock on the mantelshelf.

'There was no meat in them samwidges to-day, again,' said Jekker, taking a knife from his pocket and scraping around the bowl of his pipe with it. He flushed darkly. He had decided that Phoebe needed a lesson, and that he would give her one. The omission was probably her fault. He would give her a hiding, and have her crying when Caroline came in. That would please Caroline. He wondered where she was. His face was set in its usual expressionless mask, except for the shadow of a frown over his eyes. Throwing his knife on to the table, he rose unwillingly. Phoebe had disappeared.

In five minutes she came down the stairway, first her big, patched boots, then her dirty dress, then her large, coarse face plastered with make-up. She paused at the bottom of the steps to look at herself once more in the oblong, tin-framed mirror she had herself bought and hung there. As she turned, the man met her with a blow on the face.

'That'll learn yer not to put meat in my samwidges,' he roared.

The woman flared up with rage, and swore at him.

'It was Ca'line put 'em up,' she shouted, dodging another blow, and as he pursued her around the kitchen, striking at her with his ham-like hands, she yelled, 'An' it's the last food Ca'line'll ever put up for you, yer —'

He caught hold of her stringy hair, and held her. 'Wot d'yer mean by that?' he asked, his huge face suffused with blood.

She twisted until she could look up at him out of her angry, downward-turning eyes. 'Wot do I mean by that?' she mocked him, 'I mean she'll never come back 'ere, the bloody, pinchin' 'ellcat! I've seen to that!'

For a minute he held her by the hair and arms, while he thought. Not for a second of the time did she abate the din she was making.

'Where's my Ca'line?' he asked eventually, tightening his grip on the woman's arms.

'Your Ca'line,' she screeched, writhing with pain, 'she'll not come back to this place!' and she spat in his face.

Jekker released her hair and groped on the table for his knife. Phoebe screamed louder. Overcome by an anger he had never known before, he plunged the blade into her neck until her cries stopped. The woman looked up at him with stricken eyes, then, creeping slowly towards the clothes-horse, she pulled down the grey flannel shirt and held it to her throat.

The man stood with one hand pressing on the table top, staring dully at the woman on the floor. The wick in the lamp, which had been unattended for some time, caused a flame to shoot now high, now low, and smoke began to curl above the glass chimney.

'Get up, Phoebe,' said the man. He did not know that he was speaking in a whisper.

The woman muttered something, but her words were not distinguishable. A fold of the grey shirt fell forward softly. It was followed by no other movement. Phoebe could never tell the man now that Caroline's husband was out of gaol, that she had gone back to him. It was a long time before he knew, and then it did not seem to matter much.

The Music-Box

A WOMAN and a little boy were walking down the steep, cobbled street of a village. If they kept on walking for three miles they would come to a town, where there was a house which they wanted to find. They had seen the address in the advertisement column of the evening paper.

The woman was young. She was short, only about five feet in height, and she had small feet, of which she was very proud. The little boy had large, hazel eyes, both timid and thoughtful. He held his mother's hand. The two of them had the same expression of joyous solemnity; they were going to buy something.

The husband of the woman was called Theakstone Morphett. He was older than his wife, and worked in a stone quarry as a trimmer. He had sandy hair, and, as he only shaved once a week, on Saturdays, a growth of whisker and beard of the same glinting colour. His face was brick-red from exposure. He was a big-built man, without very much flesh, and he had a harsh, growling voice which frightened his son.

His wife had never been able to call him by his Christian name, Theakstone. It seemed to her silly, so she called him 'the father'. In the early days of her marriage, she had referred to him as 'he', or, when driven into a corner, as 'the master', but she did not like to say this often, as it was too true. She seemed thankful when her child was born, as she could at last call her husband something definite.

As the little boy, whom she christened Henry, became able to talk, he, too, referred to this man as 't'father'. The family lived in the end house of the row, where the rough road wound up to the quarries, and beyond that to the moors; and when the little boy, who was playing at some mysterious game of his, alone, saw the big man coming into sight, slowly swinging his yellow corduroy trousers with their funny, belted legs, he would run up the steps crying, 'Mother, 'ere's t'father!'

Henry could not quite make up his mind about 't'father'. The house was certainly better and quieter without this man, who sprawled in the high-backed wooden chair that had the goatskin tied over the top if it, and looked discontentedly at his small son; who often let it be known that he would have preferred a big, fat, rollicking, sandy baby to this quiet creature with questioning eyes.

But there was no need to trouble much, there were too many interesting things in the world. Every Monday was washday. Even when he was a tiny baby, Henry's mother would take him down into the cellar kitchen, underneath the living kitchen, where there was a brick-built copper for boiling the clothes in. She would light the fire with yellow-burning twigs, then a very little coal, and some coke, and soon there would be plenty of hot, soapy water. As soon as he was old enough, she would give him a little water in a pail, and let him pretend to wash something — one of the red, spotted handkerchiefs which 't'father' took his dinner in, or even his own blue and red striped shirt. And he would kneel on the stone-flagged floor, rubbing away, sometimes looking out through the small window with the flat grating above it. When he got tired of that, he would watch his mother bending over the great wooden tub, as she lifted out garments and rinsed them, and threw them with more or less accurate aim into the open mouth of the copper.

He could not bear to be far away from his mother; she was the only real part of his world. There were other children of the same age living near, but he did not feel the want of a playmate. Each Sunday his mother would take him to the tiny stone chapel, where they sat on plain wooden forms, which had lengths of red baize upon them. The forms were slippery, and sometimes the baize would writhe noiselessly to the floor.

Everything at the chapel was delightful. There was a hanging chandelier filled with gas-burners which had to be lighted, one by one, with a taper at the end of a pole, if ever the day grew too dark for the preacher to see. There was a pulpit with two lots of stairs running down from it, so that you could walk in at one side, and out of the other, if you were the preacher, and you wanted to. But the best thing of all was the music.

A harmonium was all they could afford at the chapel, and an elderly, very kind-faced woman played it. She sat with her back to the congregation, because she had no self-consciousness at all. She would slip on to the round stool in front of it, the gathers of her thick and proper skirt oozing gently over the edges; her feet would press firmly on the pedals, she would work them once or twice to fill the bellows with air, then the music would come.

The boy and his mother loved it. They sang the hymns loudly. There was one they often had. 'Toiling on' they would sing, and the harmonium seemed to add, 'Ha, ha, ha! Toiling on! Ha, ha, ha!' It was worth coming to hear, however wet the day.

Once there had been a tea at the chapel, and they had both gone. The wooden forms were now arranged round long trestle tables. Plates of potted meat sandwiches, buns, biscuits and sweet cakes stood above the short or long, old or new tablecloths that had been lent. There was a huge copper tea-urn at the top, and great cups of tea were passed from hand to hand down the long expanse of table. Someone started singing 'Be present at our table, Lord'. How they dragged it out! It seemed ages to the little boy, who had been so excited all day that he had hardly been able to eat his breakfast or dinner, and now wanted very much to begin. All the time they stood up, singing, he kept looking at the sandwich he had secretly chosen to start with; but directly grace was over, an old man with a long grey beard leaned over and almost snatched it. So the little boy sat sad and downcast, and it was a long time before he ate anything.

Although the tea had not been very pleasant, something happened afterwards which changed the whole evening. There was a small cloakroom just inside the chapel, and on the day of the tea, the precious harmonium had been moved into this place to give more room in the main hall. Here the boy found it. Furtively he tried the lid. It was open. His heart beat quickly as he put his hand on the soft-falling ivory keys. How pleasant they felt. He pulled up the chair without a back — the one used for reaching up to the cloakroom light — and sat down to play on the silent keys.

Soon he got tired of this, and began to press the pedals. As he heard the rushing sound of the air, he touched a note. It sounded loud, but the piled hats and coats all around seemed to confine the noise to this one little room. Outside, there was a confused murmur of people talking together. The tall, clean women, with their stiff white aprons and curled fringes, were clearing the long tables. He became a little bolder, and suddenly a tune played under his hand

— 'Toiling on! Ha, ha, ha!' He was frightened and happy, though however hard he tried, he could not get past the first line.

'Music!' he whispered; then he jumped up and went to look for his mother.

She was helping to wash up. He stood beside her, tugging at her skirt, and a strange woman bent over him and said, 'No boys allowed in here; go out.' He did not answer her, but stood impatiently there until his mother noticed him. He said, 'I want to whisper.'

She put down the dishcloth she had been holding, smiling apologetically at the strange woman.

'Henry wants to go somewhere,' she told her.

He waited until they were in the main hall, with its chattering crowd. Then he said, 'Come and listen to me play the harmonium!'

Guiltily they stole into the cloakroom and closed the door. The boy had a pink colour in his face, he was excited. 'Listen!' he cried.

He pressed down his feet and played his tune with confidence. Over and over again he played the first line of 'Toiling on!'

His mother leaned near him like a young girl. 'Wait a minute!' she cried, 'try this for the second line.'

Between them, miraculously, they found it. How happy they were. The noise grew louder, and their joy with it. When the door opened, and Miss Altass — the playing lady — came in, there they froze into a picture of guilt, one sitting, the other half standing.

'You mustn't touch the harmonium,' said Miss Altass, not so gently as usual. She closed and locked it. They watched her, and did not say a word, only moved quietly away.

But, afterwards, at home, they had something new to talk about. They could recall the scene a hundred times, and never tire. And one day, the little boy said dreamily, 'I wish we had some music.'

His mother had just taken the last loaf from the oven, and placed it on end on the baking-board. She pushed the warm oven-cloth under her chin and stood there thinking. The little boy looked up at her, and smiled because she was smiling. Gradually, her face grew bleak; she said, 'T'father 'ud never let us 'ave any in the 'ouse. 'E doesn't like it.'

After that she had cheered up, and between them, they made a secret. She was going to save up for a harmonium, and then they would go and buy one. It would be hard to save, because there was never much money, but she could try. Penny by penny, a little hoard grew.

Twice, 't'father' nearly discovered their secret. Once, the pot in which he kept his paper spills — spells, he called them — was empty, and he was looking everywhere for some more; and once he was looking for somewhere to hide something himself. But luckily, he did not find the money. The little boy could hardly hold in his impatience. 'Can't we go now?' he would say, almost every day.

At last, the mother got the greengrocer, who called every Thursday, to change her pennies into shillings for her. There were not many, but she thought, 'We might get an old one, that didn't cost much, and I would pay a bit every time I could save it.' She had often read notices in the brokers' windows, 'Weekly payments taken'.

It was a mild, dull afternoon in early autumn when they walked down the street. As they passed Rumsden's Mill, there was the sound of clattering machinery. Mrs Morphett had worked in a mill before she was married, and now a sudden yearning overcame her to be back among the racket of the machines. It was there she had dreamed her youthful dreams, which had not then included Theakstone Morphett. Fronting the road was a wooden door with a few holes in it, and she and the boy peered through them; they never passed without looking in. Nothing could be seen but wheels, whirling belts, and dust.

After they had looked as long as their excitement would let them, they straightened themselves and walked on, down to the valley, over the bridge by the old Venture, and up the other hillside. Mrs Morphett held in one hand a purse, containing her money, and the advertisement which she had cut out of the paper. It read, 'Musical instruments of all descriptions for sale. Unlimited choice. Apply 13 St Leonard's Terrace.'

At last they arrived at St Leonard's Terrace. For a long time the woman and her little boy did not dare to look for number thirteen, the road was so imposing. There were three-storeyed houses with big bay windows. Each had a small garden in front of it, with high, green-painted railings. Who would live in such houses but gentle-men, they thought, and were almost certain they had been directed to the wrong address. Even as they lingered, an old man came out of the gate of number thirteen, carrying a shabby violin-case. He was muttering to himself as he passed them, and tremblingly buttoning up the top button of his coat. They watched him until he had turned the corner, then they opened the gate of thirteen, and walked up to the house entrance, and knocked.

In front of them was a large door, with a great amber-coloured knob on it. Henry stared at the knob, and thought it was so beautiful that for one moment he almost forgot the object of their visit. This door opened into a small, square hall, and beyond that was another door and a long passage. A tall, thin man with a black moustache answered their knock. Mrs Morphett looked first at his waistcoat, then at her own small feet, but she did not say anything. The little boy stiffened. 'Please have you got . . .' he began, but hearing his own voice, which sounded very loud, he fell silent.

'Come forward,' said the man, speaking in a deep, rich voice. They went forward only as far as the square hall, and stopped. 'Follow me,' he continued, still in the same deep tones, and they followed him down the passage into a large, uncarpeted room. There he left them, after saying, 'Pray excuse me, I will be back in a second.'

They stood in the dark back room, amid a profusion of fiddles, harps, pianos, and all shapes and sizes of musical instruments. They did not dare to move, and stood very quiet, almost holding their breath, until the man returned.

The little boy felt very proud of his mother as she looked up into the face of the dark gentleman and said, 'How much is the harmonium?' She even managed to smile, a small, terrified smile. He thought she looked very pretty.

As soon as she heard the price, she turned and made for the door, pulling the reluctant child with her; but before they could reach it, somehow the dark gentleman was in their way. He began to smile and talk to them, he did not want them to go without buying something. He showed them a square yellow box, covered with painted red flowers. 'This,' he said, 'might be something more in your line?'

As he spoke, he lifted the box on to an old packing-case, pushed into it a roll of perforated paper, and began to turn the handle. The boy and the woman stood as stiff as statues, but entranced. Beside this, a harmonium was nothing! The first tinkling tune it played was 'The Minstrel Boy', which Mrs Morphett had learned long ago at school. She nodded her head and began to hum, her eyes shining.

'What is it, mother?' whispered the little boy.

'It's a music-box,' said his mother, 'and if it isn't too dear, we'll buy it.'

She imagined it playing for ever in the kitchen at home. They would put it on the end of the dresser, and treat it so carefully. When the grey, driving rain poured past the window, and the wind howled down from the moor, there it would be, ready to put heart into them; and afterwards, when Henry went to school — she could not bear to face that day, though it was already so near — it would always be a magnet to draw him safely back.

The man, who had been considering a price, smoothed down his moustache, and looked at them dubiously. He had intended to ask five shillings, but he put another shilling on for luck. In one corner of the room a violin-string snapped, and they started.

'You can have it for six shillings,' he said, 'and the tunes alone are worth that.'

The mother and son looked at each other, he hopefully, she happily, then they both looked at the dark gentleman, who was stifling a yawn. And a few minutes afterwards they passed again the iron railings of numbers eleven, nine, seven, five, three, and one, the woman carrying a large box inadequately wrapped, as if it were a holy thing.

They seemed to reach home in a moment. How well the box fitted its corner of the dresser, how the red flowers on its lid winked in the firelight! They played several tunes before they took off their outdoor things. His mother turned the handle while the little boy sat on his chair looking at her with solemn, ecstatic eyes. They were both serious, grave, and spoke little. Once, the mother said in a sharp, defiant voice, 'You sh'll 'ave an 'armonium next year,' although she knew it was next to impossible. The harmonium did not seem to matter so much now.

All at once they heard footsteps.

'It's t'father!' said the boy, in dismay. There was no meal ready for him.

They jumped up and ran to the door, looking like two children, flushed and happy. The little boy boldly took hold of one yellow trouser leg and cried, 'Father, father!' The man said, 'Wheer's my tea?'

'It won't be a minute.' His wife pushed the kettle into the heart of the fire and hurriedly put some things on the table.

The father seemed to be annoyed about something. He had lost a shilling that afternoon. It was not often that he put money on a horse, and, almost without exception, he lost. But he never gave up hoping that next time it would come off at a long price. All at once his glance fell on the music-box. 'What's that contraption?' he growled.

Looking at him, the little boy began to whimper. It came over him that his father was possessed of power, and that he would use it cruelly. The mother seemed to feel that way too. Shading her face with the teapot, she stood waiting for the kettle to boil. She had the look of a child waiting to be whipped.

'Come on, let's be knowin'. What's that contraption?' He was proud of the long word.

'It — it's a music-box,' she said, almost inaudibly.

He looked at it dully.

The little boy watched his father's face. Then, still whimpering, he dragged a stool to the edge of the dresser, stood up on it, and began to turn the handle.

The man listened for a minute, then a heavy anger settled on his face. 'Shut that row!' he shouted, standing up and waving his arms. ' 'Oo brought that blasted thing into the 'ouse?'

The little boy stopped turning, and as he looked at the father, the bright colour ran out of his face, leaving only a sickly pallor around his two staring dark eyes. The lid of the kettle began to shake, but the mother did not pour the boiling water into the teapot.

'I brought it,' she said. She was as white as the little boy.

'Well, you can tek it back,' said the man. He kept looking at the box indignantly, as if it had done him some injury.

The water from the kettle began to splash on to the fire; and that was the only sound to be heard in the room.

As soon as the man had set off to his work the next morning, the woman slowly dressed to go out. She buttoned the boy into his overcoat, and opened the door. There was a fog, and they both coughed as they stepped out into the street. They had not been able to eat any breakfast, and they shivered in the chill morning air.

The woman carried the music-box, wrapped and ready to go back. She had cried until she was weary, and so had the little boy. They had asked again to be allowed to keep the music-box, had promised that it shouldn't be played when 't'father' was in, but he simply said, 'Tek it back.' He could not see why his wife and son should want music when he did not.

The two walked very slowly, as the box seemed heavy. The mother was ashamed. She did not know how to approach the tall, dark gentleman; she was afraid he would not give her her money back. There was only one bright spot. She had not told her husband that the thing was paid for. Indeed, she had not had the chance, and the boy had clung to her dress, quietly, all the time her husband had shouted.

They stopped often to rest, but at last, once more, they were in St Leonard's Terrace. The tall houses were wrapped in fog, water dripped from the trees with their few twisted leaves, and the pavements were so greasy that many times they slipped and almost fell.

As his mother timidly knocked at the door, the little boy wiped the moisture from the amber-coloured knob, so that he could better see it. In doing so, he turned it, and the door opened softly beneath his hand. There was not a sound to be heard. He turned to his mother, looking up at her humbly, out of his swollen eyes. She seemed to understand him. Pushing open the door with her arm, she carefully lowered the parcel on to the floor of the little square hall, then she gently closed the door. Very soon the two figures had vanished in the fog.

The Enchanted Morning

MARY was the youngest girl, so all the clothes came down to her. Her three sisters were tall and slender, but Mary was differently made, little and round and soft, and as the dresses were buttoned on to her, they felt tight and uncomfortable under her arms and around the yokes. Mary was ten, and the three younger children were boys, who in turn had to wear each other's clothes. The money was like the clothes; it did not quite fit anywhere.

In spite of pinchings and scrapings, interspersed with silly extravagances, such as only their mother could have thought of, the family went every year to Sandlands for a month. They took a furnished house, with two bow-windows, in Avonlea Road, a row of stone-built houses, smelling of respectability. In Avonlea Road there was not one card advertising APARTMENTS hanging drunkenly from an insecure fastening above a fanlight; no window was ever opened — for fear, perhaps, that some of the respectability might escape; no charabanc ever roared lustily through the quiet retreat; no wandering minstrel turned its dusty deathliness to life.

As the boys trailed home, Indian file, each afternoon, even they desisted from scraping their wooden spades along the pavement. When they entered Avonlea Road, a hush, too, seemed to descend on their noisiness, and carefully choke it.

The walls of the backyards were seven or eight feet high, so that if ever any washing were hung out, the shame of it would not pass even so far as the next-door neighbours. Yet for Mary, there was something lovely and secret about Avonlea Road and Sandlands. For months forgotten, this would suddenly arise and be a place of eternal summer. There were no gardens to the houses, and as she passed each window she would try to look in, but mostly clean, starched curtains guarded the windows like dragons. Here and there a piano, rarely opened, shone in the gloom, or even a many-mirrored sideboard. More often only a small table with an embroidered cover, supporting a large green aspidistra plant, revealed itself to her eager eyes.

Mary was usually alone. Her eldest sister was engaged, and thus almost removed, already, from the family. The two girls who followed her, Elsie and Flora, were inseparable. Her brothers, eight and seven and five years old, found their pleasure in mechanical things. They had rather build ugly fortifications than castles decorated with fresh green seaweed and hard-sought shells. But lately, something new had happened. At the early age of ten Mary had got a sweetheart.

Elsie and Flora had sweethearts, too, and these youths had a brother of thirteen. They bribed him to go occasionally along with Mary, so that all the young people could be together, and their respective mothers would not then ask awkward questions. Stanley Perigo was a docile boy, with dreamy hazel eyes, and a thickish skin out of which grew millions of pale, gold-glinting, tiny hairs. He bought a packet of chocolate for Mary with his bribe money. She was greatly touched, and saved the silver wrappings from the chocolate as proof that she had had something given to her.

Mary lived in a world as secret and close and mysterious as Avonlea Road. At meal-times — she loved food — she would come into the everyday world, and quarrel and snatch in an unbecoming way. She would lean across the table to slap Jerry or Don, or scuffle with Norrie at her side, and she in turn would be slapped by Elsie or Flora or Janet. But whenever she wanted she could return to her secret world, where she played continually at being 'the only one'.

She had a dream father, tall and handsome and distant, not little and fat, with soft hands and a too-cheerful smile, like her real father; and a sweet-scented, bronze-haired mother who leaned over her dear only child each night to kiss her, wearing a white satin cloak over a beautiful low-cut gown in which she was going to a splendid ball, instead of the little, harassed, mouse-haired, faded woman, fretful with coming middle-age and child-rearing, who was her real mother.

One morning Mary woke up crossly. Everybody else was up, and she hated to be the last. That would mean little, perhaps no milk for her porridge, and she hated it without double quantity. The milkman did not come until after nine, and she could not bear to wait. So she pushed her bare feet into her sandals — sand- and pebble-filled as usual — after putting on her clothes and washing anyhow, and went sulkily downstairs.

Her mother was at the front door, shading her eyes with her hand, looking up the road after her boys. She turned round as she heard the little girl and noted her cross, angry stare.

'So you've got up at last, have you?' said her mother, frowning.

Mary did not answer, but went along the passage to the kitchen. Her dream mother would just now be having a cup of tea in her bedroom and opening her letters. At least, she let Mary open them with a thin, cool, ivory paper-knife, then she read them. Sometimes she read bits out loud for Mary, or laughed in her young, charming way.

'Your porridge is in the pan,' called her real mother.

Mary's heart sank. This would mean that her mother had poured what drop of milk was left into the iron pan. The porridge would be lukewarm, and it would taste funny. She scraped it into a dish and began to eat. It was horrible. She began to cry, quietly but intensely, until the tears ran into her porridge. Then she played at stretching her tongue on to first one cheek and then the other, catching her tears as they fell. This became so interesting that the tears stopped. She plastered some treacle on the crumby slices of bread lying on a plate in the middle of the table, and ate away, eyes wide open, elbows on the table, sandal heels drumming on a chair bar. A fly, one of the dozen with a temporary home upon the gas-bracket, swooped and sailed perilously near her nose.

She still wore her blank stare when her mother walked wearily into the kitchen. She was at that moment having wheat-cakes and milk from a blue bowl, and a dream nurse was saying, 'Hurry with your breakfast, Miss Mary. There's a lovely surprise waiting for you at the door.' She knew it was a white pony, and that she would ride in the park, and that her father would give her one of his rare fond looks and call her 'my daughter'.

'Elsie and Flora slipped out without giving me a hand,' her mother was saying, 'so you'll have to stay in and help me to wash up. I can't do everything. There's all the beds every day, and the meals. I'm sure it's worse than stopping at home for me. What holiday I get out of it, I don't know.'

As the words penetrated her brain, Mary pushed her plate away and gave a loud wail.

'I don't want to wash up!' she cried; 'I want to go out with the others,' and putting her hot head down among the crumbs she sniffled.

'Look here, young lady,' said her mother with some heat, 'you'll do as you're told. Get to that sink and run the water this minute. You ought to know that Elsie and Flora don't want you always tagging after them. Come here and let me pin this apron on you. And get the kitchen like a palace before I come down,' she said, as she tied on the apron, and pinned it at the front with a large safety-pin. Then she took her yawning way upstairs.

The little girl wiped her face angrily on the apron, and tackled the washing-up. She was allowed to leave the pans; but this morning, burning with a sense of injustice, she did everything. The injustice was felt, not because she had work to do, but because Elsie and Flora were going with the Perigo boys for a new long walk, and they had promised that she should go as well. They had all arranged to meet at a quarter to nine at the corner of Lovers' Lane and go exploring. They had deliberately let Mary go on sleeping, and had slipped away without doing any work. She had not even the patience to ride around the park on her dream pony. Vexation made her fingers fly.

She washed and dried all the breakfast things, rinsed the sink, and hung up the dish-cloths. Then she shook the rug and began to sweep the kitchen floor. There was no fire, and scraps of food — tomato skins and burnt crusts — lay on top of the crumbling cinders in the fireplace. She raked out the grate and carried yesterday's ashes to the bin at the bottom of the yard. The high cement walls had round red brick tops to them, and wherever a crack appeared in the cement, green moss grew. There were small plots of earth at the front of the walls where a few tender plants struggled upwards to the sunlight. She longed to get away from the gloom of tall houses.

At last the work was done, but not very well done. Things were not in their proper places. She felt angry with the housework, and pulled the safety-pin from the front of her apron, tearing her dress as she did so. Then she twisted the apron, and with hot, fumbling fingers untied the strings. All was quiet above. She called, 'I've finished', softly, but there was no reply. She crept upstairs and found her mother fast asleep on an unmade bed, her tired eyes a little open, her hands relaxed. Mary watched her for an uncomfortable moment before going down. Her mother asleep seemed to be more of a stranger than ever.

Walking silently, she locked the back door. The milk had already come, and she had taken it with uneasy hands into the cellar. Fortunately, none had spilt. Then she tiptoed to the front door, dropped the latch, banged it shut from the outside, and was in the street, free. Lest her mother should come to the window and cry after her, she flew as if with wings.

Once safely around the top corner of the road, she halted, the dust from her hasty footsteps settling around her. A bright sun shone on the left-hand houses. The murmur of the sea sounded not far away. That meant the tide was coming in. She had a longing to walk on the shore, to hurt her feet on the blue-white pebbles, the part the tide did not reach, but she knew her little brothers would be somewhere near, digging channels in the sand for the encroaching water. Always they dug, and always the water ran irresistibly up the channel until it overflowed and made their work vain. She could not understand their pleasure, their assertion and belief that they were 'making it easier for the tide to come in'.

Her crossness left her. She determined to follow her sisters on the inland road. Perhaps Stanley Perigo would be waiting for her. He had downy, pink cheeks and a round head. He had very little to talk about, but it was nice to have a sweetheart. It would be pleasant to say at school when she went back, 'I have a sweetheart called Stanley Perigo,' except that nobody would believe her, and the older girls would laugh. Yet it would be true. When they were together they walked behind the others, hand in hand, because they liked each other and were lonely. They liked to pick flowers and to pretend they were trains or motor-cars; but the older ones, who were in their teens, did not like that at all, and threatened to leave 'you blessed kids' behind if they did not behave themselves. So they were driven to playing at 'I spy', which made Mary sorry, as she always won.

Nobody was waiting for her at the trysting-place, so she turned and walked slowly down Lovers' Lane, swallowing hard to send down the lump in her throat. Nobody ever waited for her. Just at the entrance to the lane was a boneyard, and a heap of cows' horns was piled high in one corner. The place had a breath-taking, not really unpleasant, smell, but it had the effect of keeping the crowds of holiday-makers from examining too closely the interesting-looking road beyond.

The lane was muddy at its source, even in summer, and much manoeuvring was necessary to prevent the mud from tippling into one's sandal, underneath the instep. Then came Proctor's farm. The way led through the farmyard, and this always made Mary feel embarrassed, particularly when she was alone. Then the road was winding and beautiful, with little bridges over the dykes, and one big bridge over the railway lines. There were isolated houses, whitewashed and buried in flowers and trees, where a child might easily live with her dream father and mother for a month or two in the summer.

Mary gazed yearningly over each gate, hoping for an adventure, but nothing more came up to her than a large black dog, barking loudly. She dawdled, filling her sandals with dust, and stopping every few minutes to empty them. Soon she had passed all the houses. To left and right sprang tall flowering hedges. Sandlands, its rows of boarding-houses, its half-dozen hotels and two piers, vanished behind her. Larks sang in the clear morning air.

Suddenly the little girl paused and looked to the left, where a five-barred gate stood invitingly open. Wooden sleepers, sunk into the ground and rotting away, lay beyond it, leading to a faint track that seemed to promise something fresh. At length she was tempted in by the sheen of scarlet poppies springing from the pale green grass. Frail and silken and bold, though unmoving, they beckoned her in. As she wandered slowly past them, and past an overgrown quarry place, the way led her down to a grey-green marsh, sickly with meadowsweet.

The little path meandered on, following a tiny stream. Soon she was in a warm hollow, heavy with the scent of the meadowsweet. Mary shut her eyes and breathed up with slow ecstasy. The morning sun beat upon her in measured waves, pressing the air into her pores. She spread out her arms, and was a tree; lifted her face to the sun, and was a daisy; tumbled down on the cushiony grass, and for dreamlike seconds was a cloud, melting to nothingness under the hot glare.

The silence was profound. The larks had dropped back to the

fields behind. There was no one to see the solitary child as she put out her hand and gently touched the stiff spikes of grass or the lacy flowers with worshipping fingers. A bronze beetle bustled across a patch of bare earth near her, stopped, turned, and hurried off in another direction. A slight heat haze hovered above the rim of the rise.

She rose and continued her walk. The path led up the rise and then disappeared into the grass of a field. As she topped the hollow, a bush met her view, abloom with late wild roses, palest pink. In front of her was a sloping cornfield, pricked with red poppies, and still further beyond was the calm and glittering sea, blue and silver.

Mary stood and gazed. The sea moved restlessly with the force of the tide beneath it. Its surface broke into a million facets, re-formed, and broke again, so that it shimmered continually as if in some careless answer to the sun. A faint breeze touched the top of the young corn, which quivered and swayed, and every poppy bent a head to its caress. Only the roses at her side seemed brittle and hard, like china. The wandering wind at last stirred the tree, and a dozen silky petals fluttered down.

For a second's space, the child was a goddess. She trembled with the shock of vision. As her heart responded, her eyes filled with strange new tears. Slowly she turned, and without a backward glance retraced her footsteps. The dell of meadowsweet seemed homely and familiar, but belonging to yesterday; the quarry place, with its hanging greenery, an old friend, seen long ago. She jumped on and off the sleepers, up, down, up, down, as she had always done before. A longing came upon her to see a human face.

She ran along the road until she came to Proctor's farm, then, as usual, walked through the yard apologetically, back to the lane that was always muddy, and past the boneyard. She reached the little seaside town, filled now with smells of cooking, and discovered that she was hungry. She was no longer angry with her sisters; her face was bright with some inward content.

Avonlea Road was just the same, prim-faced, and engaged in minding its own business, not at all surprised that the sunshine was leaving the left-hand side for the right. The three little boys, in washed blue coats and trousers, were turning in at the front door of number twenty-six. One of them carried in his hand a length of seaweed like brown silk ribbon.

Again at the top of the road the child paused, as if bracing herself for something. Then, 'I won't forget', she said clearly; and soon the sound of her running footsteps shattered the crystalline silence of Avonlea Road.

Frost in April

THE farm of Harry Inn Corner stood high and alone on a moorland shoulder. It faced west. On its south side rose an untidy stone shed, called the mistal, in which twenty cows were housed, and behind it was a grey-green, neglected garden, where coarse grass grew in uneven clumps. Just in front of the house a stony road ran, twisting to the right within sighting distance, continuing downhill until it found a sanctuary of trees, and there, apparently, vanishing. To the left, it ran an unseen distance of three miles, up and down the inhospitable shoulder, hedged with wind-blown thorns and black, forgotten brambles, past only Joyts and Pennypot — farms a field's length from the lane — until it joined the main road for Farchester at Starting Post.

The wife of the farmer was a little woman, with a red, tight-drawn skin, and great, brown, terrified eyes. She started in a painful way at any sound from the outside world, yet she always spoke loudly, repeating what she said two, and sometimes three times, 'You gi' me a fright; I say, you gi' me a fright.' The jerky ticking of the octagonal wall-clock was the only noise she seemed really to understand, and to draw comfort from. She would stare at the clock when in any predicament, all the time softly stroking the sheepskin rug which was tied on the back of a wooden chair. She seemed to be subject to some fear which never left her, and which solitude increased slowly but inevitably.

She had six great, broad sons, inarticulate, like the animals they tended, and after them, a daughter. Tildy, short for Matilda, had been a pretty baby, with a crown of tangled bronze curls, very hard to tend. She had small, oblique blue eyes, and a voice as clear as a thrush's. But she had very little to say, keeping her voice only to sing with. She inherited the tight-drawn, red skin of her mother, rough to the touch and scaly; yet she had some hidden charm that drew a second glance. Occasionally, the moorland wind hurt her eyes, making them red and sore, and she would look away when speaking to anybody.

Tom Morris, the father, appeared to be the only normal member of the family. He was a neat man, with straw-coloured hair and moustache, a very pleasing tenor voice, and a fondness for breeding canaries. He sang in the chapel choir, and had a religious bias. Yet, seeing him in the farm kitchen, humming to himself as he wiped his hands on the soiled towel near the sink where the pump was, you might have found in him an answer to a strange riddle. He loved his canaries, and his singing practice, and made a great show of working hard at the farm; but if there was any labour that could be put on to another's shoulders, he would contrive to do it in a way that was not, at first glance, discernible.

The six sons, uncouth lads, grew up into strong, heavy men. As soon as they were of an age, they married and left home, with just enough knowledge and ambition to be labouring hinds for other men. They seemed eager to leave the farm in which they were born and reared, and never returned even so much as for a visit at Christmas, or Easter, or other festival. If they had cared for their baby sister, they never showed it; but sometimes the little girl and her mother would set off and call on the nearest ones, and play with their sturdy children, and turn back home as darkness fell.

The youngest son had done well for himself. He had married an idiot girl whose grandmother had died and left her five hundred pounds and a house of furniture. His brothers envied him, because he need only work for two or three days a week. But the idiot girl proved prolific, and with a steadily increasing flock of children, he found that in spite of his wife's wealth, he would have to look for regular work. Everybody in the district was well supplied, so with a sinking heart he returned to work for his father. Marriage and money had a little armed him, and while his father offered him the barest pittance for wage, he on his part stipulated that he should not arrive at the farm before six o'clock, until after the morning milking was over, and the milk in the cans all ready to take to the station. He did not often work near the house.

With the sons and men away, and the girl now seventeen, life should have been easier for Mrs Morris; but it never was. The house was a large one. There was an unused parlour, stuffy with inherited lumber; and earth-smelling from the green plants which entirely filled the small window space. There was a large living kitchen, the floor of which constantly echoed to the clatter of iron-rimmed footwear. There were stone-floored sculleries, pantries, and passages, all to scrub interminably, besides the upstairs rooms, and the noisy, voracious, dirt-making birds in the attic. The house was always spotless, the result of unceasing labour. The farm mistress's little leisure was spent in mending torn clothing, seated in a chair beneath the great paraffin lamp which hung from the centre of the dark ceiling.

Again, the poultry was spread far and wide, and the two women had it all to tend. The poultry houses were in sheltered corners of the various fields, and it was a long way from one to another. Some of the hens were kept near to the house, and were continually squawking and flying heavily from under impatient feet into the bare branches of the few meagre trees, then back to the ground. The cows were shut up from October to May, and their gentle lowing, deep and true as an organ note, instead of breaking the silence, seemed to make it more profound.

Work at the farm began early and ended late. Winter was a cruel time. Sometimes, as Tildy carried the forty great pails of water from the well in the road to the shippen, two for each cow, the child would pause, and pressing her numbed hands into her armpits, would look around her at the frozen hill-tops, and unknown desires would burst into bloom in her thin bosom, only to die as she heard her father's voice asking how much longer she was going to stand there 'gapin' at nowt'. The farmer far preferred sitting milking, with his head against the warm flanks of Bess or Beauty, to carrying the water in.

The dapper little farmer was proud of his daughter's capacity for work, and also of her sweet, clear voice. As soon as she was old enough, she went with him into the chapel choir, and even two or three nights a week to practise singing. The long walk to Starting Post and back home they reckoned as nothing; indeed, they never thought of it, or dreamed of putting off a practice, no matter how bad the weather. This was innocent joy. Meantime the mother would sit listening to the tock, tick-tock of the wall-clock, her eyes wide with fear, her ears alert for alien sound. But her life was set, planned for her by her husband, and she dared not deviate from his ways. He was a miser.

At seventeen, Tildy's rebel curls had fallen into an orderly beauty. Her eyes were much stronger, and she could now, if she wished, stare back into other eyes, but the force of habit was too strong in her, and usually she looked away when addressing anybody, and appeared to be thinking of other things. Her mouth had a droop to it; she suffered much from backache, yet she did not complain, except very rarely to her mother. When she felt worse than usual, her mother would go out into the howling wind, rain or bitter frost of the winter's dawn, and carry the heavy pails of water to the patient cattle, while her father sat snug and warm behind a cow and sang, 'Come unto Me, all ye that labour,' in a voice sweet enough to draw tears from the eyes of the devil himself.

It would have been easy for him to have had water laid on from the well to the byre, he was always going to do it, but he could not bear to spend the money. He grudged the coal on the fire, the butter on the bread. He grudged his son the few shillings he paid him, and never gave his daughter a penny. Yet he was a very pleasant man to talk to. When his friends came to look at his canaries they envied his home, his birds, his cattle, his poultry. They knew he was close, yet they envied him even for that, saying he would have a tidy bit laid by. Before their eyes, Tildy mixed food for the poultry, or cleaned the byre, or swilled out the yard, clad in a thick grey frock, with a little fringed shawl tied over her hair; singing, though her hands were red and swollen.

In the summer of her nineteenth year, after the haymaking was over and done with, she met Irving Barr, and they fell in love; not so much in love as in ecstasy. He was tall, over a foot higher than she was, with a clear, tanned skin, under which the blood flowed easily. He, too, had blue eyes, but they were large and full, and his lips and nostrils were clear-cut as a statue's. His hands were smooth, strong, and small; they did not look like a farmer's hands. He had come with his newly-widowed mother from over the hills by Adderthwaite, to an easier farm near Starting Post, known as Jonah's Eye. They were having everything up to date at Jonah's Eye, even a bathroom, unknown luxury. He was twenty, and unaware of his own good looks and the effect they had on the village girls.

First, he heard Tildy's voice in the choir. She was singing a solo. From under an unfashionable hat her curls cascaded. She was looking into a dusty corner of the chapel as though she saw an angel there, and her clear voice broke through her lips like a singing spring. Not a muscle of the young man's face moved, yet at that moment he had determined that only this girl should be his wife. As she finished singing, she brought her glance to his, and for some seconds, their looks embraced in a shaft of summer sunlight.

He tried hard to become acquainted with her, but by some means her father always managed to put him off. Mr Morris would talk affably with him, and contrive to send Tildy home before he had a chance to say one word to her. He was baffled by the unseen barrier. There was no reason for it. Here was a man with a daughter, here was a young man who wanted in a right and proper way to come courting that daughter. Yet Mr Morris smiled and chatted, even invited him to see the canaries, but always saw to it that Tildy had no opportunity of talking to him. It was simple enough to other people. Tom Morris did not want to part with his hard-working daughter.

One night, as she was going to bed in her little room over the front passage, the girl heard a low, sweet whistle. She flushed, and, pulling on her dress, leaned out of the window. To the still figure beneath her in the garden she whispered, 'Hush! Oh, please, please be quiet; father'll hear you!'

For answer, the young man looked up at her earnestly, and saying, 'Good night' in low tones, he turned from her, strode through the neglected garden, vaulted the wall, and was gone. She watched him as long as she could see him in the dusk, and as she climbed into her bed, she hid her smiling face in her hands and hoped she would dream about him.

Sometimes he came to wish her good night, and sometimes he did not. She would stand in her room, not daring to undress until there was no further likelihood of his coming. They grew to exchanging a word or two, then they talked; the fear of being found out adding a delicious zest to their conversations. One night he persuaded her to climb out of the window, and they spent a fearful yet happy half-hour walking up and down the field.

'Why can't I come for you in the evenings and take you out?' he asked. 'There's no reason why you shouldn't come.'

'Perhaps if you asked father he'd let me,' she suggested.

The following Sunday the young man asked the older one if he could come courting Tildy.

'I'm afraid my girl's too young,' he answered with a deprecating smile. 'She's only seventeen.'

'Nineteen,' corrected the young man, unguardedly.

'Seventeen,' answered the father coldly, giving him a deadly smile. 'Somebody must have been informing you wrong.' And he would not say any more.

'It's no use, Tildy,' Irving said, as they walked the lane late that night. 'He thinks you're too young.'

'Don't vex him,' she said imploringly; and turned back to go home.

Winter put an end to many of their meetings, but their love grew steadily. The young man went to chapel each Sunday, and there they were able to steal glances at one another, all through the long service. Always on Sunday nights, unless snow was on the ground and his footmarks could be seen, he came to kiss her cold, frightened lips, and to wish her good night. At times he grew wildly angry because of her father; he wanted to climb up into her little room.

'Oh, no!' she cried, because she was terrified — not afraid of him, but afraid that he should see the ill-furnished little place, with its wooden chest in place of dressing-table, and tin box in place of chair. 'You mustn't say you'll come in, or I'll never open the window to you again!'

'Well, let me kiss the pillow where you put your head,' he said; and he would not be content until she brought her pillow for him to kiss.

One evening in spring, the girl asked her mother if she could go out. The father was away, and they did not expect him back until late. Her mother stared at her, and all at once put a trembling hand on her arm. She said, 'Go out, Tildy, I say go out, Tildy, before he comes. But get back before he comes back, or else —' She did not say or else what, but Tildy knew.

She met Irving as they had arranged. They walked over the far hill and up on to the moors, where last year's heather crackled beneath their feet. They talked and kissed as they walked, and could not bear to turn their footsteps homeward; but at last they had to do so.

'I shall come back again to kiss you good night and to see that everything's all right,' he said, as they parted, not too near the house.

When she entered the kitchen, pretty and flushed and warm, her father was waiting for her. He had his hat on, and there was a stick laid across his knees. In the opposite doorway her mother was standing, holding her left hand up to her cheek. The girl hung back, her face paling.

'Come here, Tildy,' said her father, softly smiling, and still smiling, he pinioned her hands behind her back and beat her until she screamed. Half his blows fell on the girl and half on her mother.

When the girl went up to her room she opened the window wide. Then she lay down on her bed, wiping away her tears with a rough cotton handkerchief. She did not get up when she heard a low whistle, nor was she afraid when her lover came and gently kissed her wet eyelids.

Hay-time came round again. The lovers, each busy throughout the day, thought constantly of one another. He bought her a little ring with a blue stone in it, and she wore it all night long. He bought her, too, a wedding-ring, but she could think of no safe place to hide it, and wore it tied round her middle with a piece of string. 'You'll soon be wearing it,' he told her confidently. 'As soon as you're twenty-one — and perhaps before that — we're going to be married. I don't care how soon.'

'And neither do I!' she answered joyfully. 'I don't care, whatever happens.'

There was just one thing they had forgotten. In late summer he caught a chill. A night passed, and he did not come; then two nights, three, four, five; and on the sixth, she heard from her father that he was dead.

Tom Morris had come in and sat down at the table. He had seemed full of inward pleasure about something. He began to eat, and to talk to the womenfolk. 'Yes,' he said, 'young Barr's dead. His mother's telling everybody that he's been out night after night wi' some lass or other, and caught his death of pneumonia.'

Tildy watched the movement of her father's jaw as he chewed his food and told the tale of her lover's death, with malice, with amusement. How much did he know as he told it? She rose abruptly from the table, and went upstairs into her room. She stood near the window, looking out into the pale blue sky. There was a pink reflection from the sunset. She did not see it. She had not yet realized the full meaning of her father's words, only that something dreadful, unspeakable, had happened to her.

She heard the sound of footsteps, and turned blindly to hold the door. She was too late; her mother had crept into the room. She put her hand on her daughter's hair and whispered. 'Don't take on, Tildy, I say, don't take on.'

The girl did not move. She said with difficulty, 'Does father say he's dead?'

Her mother did not answer; only stroked the girl's hair.

'It is true? Have *you* heard?' she asked sharply, watching her mother's eyes.

The old woman nodded. 'I've known sin' dinner-time,' she said.

The girl shook off her mother's hands.

A week later, Tom Morris again went away. He had whistled and sung all the week long and did not appear to have a care in the world. As soon as he was gone the girl put on a long black coat of her mother's. It had great pouched sleeves and much material in it, and would have looked a caricature of a coat on anybody less scared and sad. Then she put on a black hat of her own.

'I'm going, mother,' she said.

Her mother was manifestly afraid. 'I s'll be that uneasy until you come back,' she said. 'Promise me, Tildy, you won't do anything rash. I wish I could come with you.'

'Oh, mother, do come! Lock up and come. I daren't go without you. Put on your black shawl. We'll hurry back as soon as we've seen it. If you're not with me, I don't know what'll happen.'

She had gathered a few late wild flowers, and, holding these tenderly in her hand, the girl went with her mother to the grave-yard and saw her lover's grave. Her mother looked about to see that nobody was near as she hid her few blossoms close to the earth, beneath the conventional hothouse wreaths which were already withering. The pale yellow October sun, about to vanish behind a cloud, threw its last beams on the two women, who hurried through their sad task as if they were thieves at work. Then they stood up, and, with their faces hidden, turned towards home.

As they entered the yard, nothing was changed. The hens still flew heavily and protestingly into the branches at their approach, then out again. A cow lowed; then another, and another; and again the silence was deeper.

Tildy changed into her grey dress, tied the little fringed shawl over her head, and made the first of her trips from the well to the byre. As she carried the heavy buckets, she slowly lifted her gaze from the stony path beneath her feet until it rested among the stars.

She had not before realized that one could see so far.

Accident

A WOMAN was sitting in a café about eleven o'clock one morning, taking sips from a cup of weak tea and eating a cream bun, without knowing she was doing so. She had a bad headache.

On the chair by her side — there were four chairs altogether around the table — she had placed a pair of thin brown gloves and a handbag. She kept looking at these from time to time. They were smeared with drying blood, as was the front of her dress; and each time she looked at them she groaned audibly.

Two waitresses, not yet in their uniforms, still occupied with cleaning out the café, ready for the lunch-hour rush, kept peering at her from the door of the kitchen. Every now and then the cook joined them, and they all cast puzzled glances at their solitary customer, eating and drinking like an automaton.

The name of this woman was Mrs Leveritt. She was between forty and forty-five years of age, and had brown eyes and a clear skin. Normally, she would have colour, but just now her face was drawn and pale. She did not seem to notice the waitresses or the cook, but was utterly possessed with one inward thought, to the exclusion of anything else.

She had a husband and three children. Not having married until she was almost thirty, her children were still quite young — indeed, they were all at school. Her husband was a joiner. She had married him because he had come after her for several years, and she liked him.

When she was young, she had been full of romance, a very high-handed girl. She wasn't going to marry anybody just for the sake of getting married. She was going to wait until somebody came with whom she could fall in love. She knew exactly how it would happen; she would see him, know him in a moment. This would be the man for whom she would leave father, mother, and home. There would be no mistake; they would both know.

But first her mother died, then her father. Fred Leveritt, who came to the house every Wednesday and Saturday — pretending to come for her father's sake, but really, she knew, to see her — had told her that the best thing she could do was to marry him. She was very fond of Fred, he was most kind, and he thought the world about her. So she had married Fred.

How calm and happy her life had been with him. She looked no older than when she was married. Her three children had suffered only from minor ailments, except Phyllis, the eldest, who had once had to go to hospital with fever. Their home was comfortable. Fred had made a great deal of the furniture, and she kept it polished bright and shining. Every year, for one week, they went to the seaside with the children, and had a good time, whether the weather was wet or fine.

This morning she had set off, soon after getting the children to school, to do some ordinary shopping. She wanted to make a steak and kidney pie for dinner. Just as she got to the cross-roads she saw there was an accident.

She had been looking into a shop window as she walked on and did not actually see the accident happen. But there was a lorry, and a boy with a sick white face climbing out of the driver's seat; and, on the ground, some yards away, a man was lying.

Mrs Leveritt's first impulse was to run away. Indeed, her feet actually turned, and when she came to her normal, kindly senses, she was going rather rapidly in another direction. With just such another whirl, she turned; and she was the one on whose knee the injured man's head was pillowed, and hers was the face on which he looked as he opened his eyes.

What happened next, Mrs Leveritt was not sure. There must have been a crowd of people, and the boy coming limping up out of the lorry, and a policeman somewhere. There must have been sombody ringing up in the nearby telephone-box for an ambulance, because soon one came.

But for Mrs Leveritt, and the man whose head she held in her arms, there was a moment of complete understanding. It was as if the world had stopped around them, and they were enclosed in a lovely crystal ball, looking for ever into each other's eyes, made perfect by love.

The crystal ball burst with a crash. Before she could draw her thoughts again into focus, everything had disappeared; the man, the ambulance, the policeman, the crowd. She had not seen the accident happen, therefore she was of no use as a witness. She walked a long way before, at last, she entered the café and ordered tea. The waitress put some stale cakes near her, and she ate mechanically.

At last she had to go home. Realizing that there was no time to make the pie, she hastily prepared a plainer dinner for the children, looked after their needs, and sent them off to school again.

In the evening, after her husband had come home and had his meal, a knock came at the door. She was washing up. Hastily drying her hands on her apron she ran to open the door. She was expecting a message. She knew not what, nor when it would come, but that it would reach her she was certain.

However, it was only Ted Rhodes, a friend of Fred's. Ted was also a joiner, but he was mostly on outside work, and was often a little stiff with rheumatism. The two men smoked and talked, and, for some reason, as soon as her work was done, the woman sat and listened to every word attentively. At the same time the other half of her brain was wondering when she could go to the hospital to visit the injured man, and if they would let her see him.

Suddenly Ted said, 'A mate o' mine was run over with a lorry this morning and killed. Kitson, 'is name was. Lived over other side 'o Shawford, near brickworks.'

Fred didn't know him.

Mrs Leveritt gave a great sigh. Here was the message.

'What was he like?' she asked, twisting her lips into a solemn smile.

'Like? Let me see,' said Ted. He thought for a minute. 'A tall chap, wi' greyish 'air and plenty o' colour. D'you know 'im?'

'I think so,' she answered, very quietly.

A tall chap, with greyish hair and plenty of colour. That was all she had to remember. And he had gone out into the dark, taking her love with him.

Blackberry Day

MRS HILLIWELL and her husband Ben sat on a seat high on the moor above Baildon, at peace with the whole world apparently, eating an early lunch. It was not much after eleven o'clock on an October morning, but the long walk they had already taken had made them hungry; so there they sat, looking contentedly before them at the clear view shining greyish-green and gold under a pale sun, and eating beef sandwiches.

Between them on the seat was a brown-paper parcel into which they kept dipping, and a drinking-cup without anything in it. There was also a small piece of yellow soap and a handbag. Nobody disturbed them, although it was Sunday, and a fine day for walking, so they ate away huddled up and warm in their thick clothing, occasionally stamping their feet, which were beginning to feel the cold, on the ground, or knocking their boots one against the other desultorily.

Though they sat there so placidly, all was not well with one of them, and that one was Mrs Hilliwell. She was sixty-two, and her husband two years younger. They had had four children, three boys and a girl, now all married. Ever since their wedding-day, nearly forty years ago, they had pulled together for one end; that when they were sixty they would retire from work.

Not that Mrs Hilliwell went out to work. All she did was stay at home, have the children, wash, bake, clean, look after Ben when he was ill, and generally run the house. She was a very good needlewoman, and even found time for a deal of crochet-work, so that there was not one cover in the house, sideboard, dressing-table, or chair-back that had not its deep edging of lace.

She was very proud of her house, and however hard they saved up for eventual retirement, never stinted that of anything. In the bedroom beside the bed with its heavy, homemade patchwork quilt, they had a real suite of shiny yellow furniture; a wardrobe with a glass in the door, a dressing-table covered with crocheted mats, and a large wash-hand stand supporting all the china on its marble top. In the middle stood the jug and bowl, wreathed about with cornflower blue roses and pink forget-me-nots. Flanking these were two inverted chamber-pots, then followed the smaller articles; a speckless soap-dish that had not yet held any soap, and an equally innocent toothbrush holder, all of the same flowered pattern.

Behind the principal bedroom was the small room that had been Ada's, and above the two was a large attic, in which had slept the three boys. Downstairs was a kitchen, a small scullery with a sloping roof — it was under the stairs, in fact — and a front room, used only at Christmas and occasionally on Sundays, containing green plush chairs and an unused walnut piano. The last owner of the house had been a decorator, and he had painted blue dragons and urns like stewpots all over the ceiling, and on the panels of the doors; when selling the house he had impressed it on them that this was 'very artestic', and as they believed him, they had never thought to have it cleaned off. This room was always very cold, because the front door opened out of one corner of it. Mrs Hilliwell prudently ran a strip of coconut matting from the kitchen door across the room to the front door, to save the carpet.

Because their house, an end one, was chilly, they had built a large, frosted-glass porch, called 't'veranda', and for many years it smelt of new wood, varnish, and dead geraniums; but it did help to keep the cold out. The house was their own, and they had come up to it by degrees, first having a cottage or two, then what is known as a 'side-scullery', and at last, some twenty years ago, a genuine 'through'.

In spite of this large house, and the grand, unused furniture, they had saved money out of Ben's weekly wage. They had elderly friends who were 'retired couples', and when they were younger had often taken the children to visit them. The man generally had a 'bit o' gardin' or a toolshed with a lathe in it, or a 'few poultry'. Whatever hobby these retired couples had, they managed to make money by it. Their more shiftless neighbours might call them tight-fisted old beggars, but everybody felt that it must be grand to have a real income that you didn't have to work for.

So Ben and Betty Hilliwell took these couples as models, were frugal without being mean, and saved without actually scraping;

and at last they had saved up enough, and become themselves the retired couple they had so often longed to be. By now they had had a month of it; a month in which to tell envious friends that they had 'retired'; to show them the silver teapot that had been bought for Ben at the conclusion of his long service as overlooker in one mill; and to plant in them the seeds of ambition.

They sat mildly eating, now and then making a remark as to the visibility, but under it all the mind of Mrs Hilliwell was seething. It had just occurred to her that it was *Ben* who had retired, *Ben* who was reaping the reward, *Ben* who was enjoying himself, and not she. What was the difference? The children were married, and there was certainly less to do, but hadn't she to get up as usual every morning, light the fire, make the breakfast, go out shopping? Still to clean, hadn't she, and wash and bake, with the added disadvantage of Ben sprawling all over the place, under her feet most of the time? Once or twice she had spoken sharply, and Ben had opened his eyes and his mouth, paused in preparing the tobacco for his pipe, and said, 'Na, lass, what's to do?' in some astonishment. She had not replied.

They were fond of walking, but elderly couples do not go walking day after day for pleasure. Ben was wondering whether to get an allotment garden, and hesitating because he had always worked in warm, steamy rooms at the mill, and caught internal colds very easily. So he only played with the thought.

They finished their food, screwed up the paper, and threw it under the seat. There was the sound of running water somewhere near. A spring tumbled out of the moorside, was caught in a stone trough, ran over the side of this and cut a passage through the heather. They took their cup to the spring, drank some water, and then Mrs Hilliwell washed her hands with the piece of soap she had brought.

'Me mother allus used to bring some soap when we went for a picnic,' she told her husband. He had heard so many times before, but he just said gravely, 'Yes'.

She dawdled for a long time, splashing her hands about in the water, so that Ben spoke sharply. 'Come on, lass. It's gettin' cold. Stop that diddlin' and' daddlin', an' let's get on wi' t'walk.'

'Get on yerself,' she said, with some resentment. 'I'm going to pick some blackberries.' There were a few bushes near, on which she had seen berries shining.

'Blackberries?' he echoed. 'Ye'll find no blegs there.'

He stumped off on to the road. In front of him, on the left, was a small stone chapel, and people began to walk out of this, and to stare at him. He did not like the way they looked at him, so he shouted in a loud voice: 'Come on, lass. Hurry up.'

It just happened that he had climbed a small hill to get on to the road, and his wife was still hidden in the hollow. Once she had peeped up to see where he was going, but noticing that the chapel was emptying, she had hidden herself again until all the people should have gone. In her pocket she had found a paper bag, and she was busy filling it with the best blackberries she could find. When she heard her husband's voice she only smiled, but there was an angry gleam in her eye. 'Let 'im wait' she thought, and went on filling her bag.

As soon as the people from the chapel had disappeared, she climbed leisurely up on to the road, holding the bag of berries loosely in her hand. She looked about her, at the isolated chapel, at the sky, at the distant view, at anything but the darkening face of her husband.

'What d'ye mean by this?' he blustered. 'Leavin' me stood 'ere to be stared at like a bloomin' flaycrow?'

'I didn't leave ye,' she said. 'Ye went by yersen. Ye should ha' stayed wi' me pickin' blackberries till t'folk 'ad passed.'

He was beside himself with cold and anger, and having to wait for a woman — he who had bossed women for so many years at work.

She held up the bag and continued, 'There's a lot of good ones in this.'

'Th'art lyin',' he said. 'Th'ast got no blegs. And i' future, th'ad best come when tha's called, or it'll be worse for thee.'

As his wife looked at him, two sparks seemed to light in her eyes. Here was a good excuse to vent her feelings. She tore open the bag, showed her husband the fine berries, and before he could say a word, pitched the lot into the graveyard over the chapel wall. She could scarcely speak for rage. All the things she had been thinking for weeks came to the surface, and as soon as she recovered her voice she railed and shouted at her husband, and he shouted back at her.

Luckily for both of them, nobody was in sight. The sun shone, yellow and tranquil, on the midday scene; on the stone chapel, the moor top, the haze of smoke over the distant city; and on the two elderly, comfortably dressed people quarrelling with each other.

'We'll 'ave no more of it, then,' Mrs Hilliwell screamed breathlessly. 'Sittin' on y'ur backside all day long while I work me 'ands off. I've 'ad enough, ye c'n get another woman to wait on ye, I'm tired. An' we'll do the thing right, we'll 'ave a divorce!'

Her husband stood listening. His mind did not work quickly; neither did his voice, but at every pause he said something.

'That'll suit me,' he cried, as soon as there was a decent lull. 'Ye wasteful creature, throwin' them good berries away. I've a good mind to make ye get ower t'chapel wall and fetch 'em all back. Now come on, damn ye, don't stand shoutin' for all Baildon to 'ear.'

'Oh, damn me!' echoed his wife. 'Then damn ye an' all. I niver 'ad such language spoken to me sin' I wa' wick, and I'm not goin' t'ave it now. I'm off.'

She was less and lighter than her husband, and she began running in front of him, carried away by her temper. She had an umbrella dangling from her left arm, and it kept bumping against her leg, but she did not try to stop it. She headed straight for the long main street of the village, where they were both known.

For some time her stout husband ambled after her, calling out to her to wait for him. His anger had evaporated, and he was sorry that he had sworn at his wife. He could not understand why he had done so, as this had never before happened in all the years of their married life. He reflected that she'd be in a rare tantrum now. Her anger, though slower to form, was always more lasting. Only once did Betty turn round, then it was to glare at him and say in a spent voice, 'I'm off home. Don't foller me!' She was stepping out like a twenty-year-old, head well up, back straight. He couldn't help admiring her.

He called out, 'Don't go so fast, lass, ye'll be rare an' poorly tomorrow.'

'I'll not,' she flashed back. 'Not for you to see, for I'll lock t'door on ye.'

They hurried down the village street with twenty yards between them, their faces set and stiff. Inwardly, Betty was more conscious of feeling happy than she had been for some years. Her sister lived in one of the cottages built high above the main road, and she knew that Martha spent a lot of her time looking out of the window.

Sure enough, Martha came out of the door as if in answer to her thought and leaned over the iron railings. She called out to her sister, 'What's up, lass? Art runnin' a race, or summat? Wilt come in for a minute?'

Betty never paused in her stride. 'Not today,' she replied, without turning her head, as if she were answering a hawker. Almost she felt that there was a race, and that she was winning. At the same time, she was trembling with fatigue, and was nearly breathless, and did not know how she would manage to get home, as there were three or four miles yet to walk.

Ben came abreast of Martha's house. He looked up to see a grin of pure happiness cross his sister-in-law's face. She pointed to Betty, sprinting down the hill.

'What's up wi' yon silly bitch?' she asked.

'Nay,' answered the husband, stopping to wipe his face, 'she's getten t'nark all right. Pitched a bag o' good berries over a wall and says she's bahn to divorce me.' He started forward again as he saw that Betty had gained a yard or two.

Off he went, leaving his sister-in-law Martha leaning on the railings outside her house, rocking herself to and fro, and wiping tears of mirth out of the corners of her eyes with a blue apron. And the sun shone kindly down on those two figures trotting, one in front of the other, along the road to eternity.

The End of the Queue

A BOY of fourteen jumped out of bed as soon as he heard his mother's voice calling 'Jonty' from the bottom of the attic stairs. The bed was opposite the dormer window, through which only an expanse of dull grey sky was to be seen. He shouted 'I'm coming', in a voice so loud that his younger brother, who slept in the same bed, woke with a convulsive start and sat suddenly upright, his eyes and mouth opened wide in surprise and fear. Jont took no notice of the little boy, but after placing a red wooden chair under the window, climbed on to it and put his face through the small square that was open.

He could see some shining grey roofs, a hen-house in a field, a length of iron railing, and two or three pools in the road beneath him. 'It's raining,' he said, in a very quiet, disappointed way.

'Oh,' answered his brother, who had been sitting up in the same dazed manner since the noise had first awakened him; and he lay down again immediately, put his knees up to his chin, and was asleep in a minute.

The elder boy, whose name was Jonathan, but who was never called anything but Jont or Jonty, got dressed in the clothes which he had put ready for himself very neatly. This morning was the beginning of a new life for him. He had left school, and was now going to help his father in what was known as 'the business'. He had been dreaming during the night of colossal tasks that had been set for him, over which he was taking more time than was humanly possible. And he was glad to wake up, to jump out of bed, and to look quickly through the window.

There seemed to be a fresh meaning in life. The very sound of his feet padding down the creaking attic stairs was different. He could not wait for the water in the tap to run warm, but washed himself in cold, so impatient was he to be off to work.

Downstairs, his father was already bent over a basin of porridge and treacle, the drooping points of his grey moustache dark with moisture. The boy had a great respect for his father, and felt proud when he thought that every day, now, he would walk at his side into town, up the steps where 'the business' was, into the dim little office, and be a sort of prince under his father, the king.

At school, he used to boast of 'our place', because there were so many boys whose fathers just went out to work for wages. There was something romantic in being able to take boys into the warehouse, to sniff up the pervading smell of leather, to point out the long rows of shoe boxes with their bronze labels showing Daisy or Beeko or Candid brands; and to steal quietly up to the far end, where there was the tiny gas-lit office with the glass window opening into the warehouse, near which his father usually sat.

For some reason unknown to the boy, his mother had been crying, and she moved about in silence, stopping every now and then to rock with her foot an old-fashioned brown wooden cradle in which a very small, delicate baby was lying.

'How's Ronald?' he asked in a whisper, pulling out a chair and sitting down on it.

'Put your boots on, do,' answered his mother. 'How many times must I tell you not to walk about the bare oilcloth in your stockings? Ronald's had a very poor night.'

'Oh,' he said, in imitation of his father's manner, 'dear me.' And he began eating his breakfast, looking out of the windows and watching the thin rain dropping into the shallow pools on the path, or following the course of a leaf falling from one of the higher trees. There were many wet, yellow leaves already lying about. At the same time, without haste, he pushed his feet into his boots which were under the table.

The new life did not seem to be beginning very well. There was not much difference here from any other day. He might have been getting ready for school, for all his mother seemed to care. She went about in an unsmiling way, preparing food for the delicate baby. Even the fire was dull and comfortless. The coal caked together, black and sulky, only opening here and there to show a meagre streak of red.

So the boy ate, and imagined himself grown up, say eighteen or nineteen. The boxes on the warehouse shelves gleamed and shone. The little office was transformed. There was even electric light and a radiator in it, and bright new ledgers in green and red bindings.

He saw himself sitting in a swivel chair, whizzing first one way and then the other. A young boy was calling him 'Sir'. He smiled secretly.

His mother came out of the door at the cellar-head, carrying a shovel with a small quantity of coal on it.

'We shall have to get some more coal,' she said, looking across at her husband. 'You'd better call at Scott's on your way down.'

Her husband turned and looked at her, but he only said 'Hannah!' quietly.

'I don't care.' She raised her voice and then looked towards the cradle. 'We shall have to get some more,' she repeated stubbornly.

The father and son set off as soon as they were ready, Jonty walking under a large umbrella with a yellow handle which his father held up. Some of their neighbours were already setting off. They looked with smiling surprise at the boy under the umbrella, who was short for his years. He wore a school cap over his fair hair, and his knees showed mottled between the tops of his socks and his short trousers. He was walking carefully, avoiding the puddles as well as he could, trying all at once to become grown up and to behave as his father did. He even assumed the distant, yet worried expression that was on his father's face.

As they passed one house, a big, black-haired boy with a heavy jowl came to the window, pulled a face, and surreptitiously shook his fist at the pair. Jont flinched, and shrank a little closer to his father's side, putting out his hand so that it touched a damp pocket flap. But after a second he moved away, turned round, and stuck out his tongue at the jowled lad, as a gesture of defiance. 'After all,' he thought, 'I go to work now. I'm not a kid any longer.' And it seemed to him that he was already a man, past being bullied in any way whatsoever.

The warehouse felt cold. There was nothing for him to do after he had lit the stove and swept up the dirty floor. He wanted very much to tidy all the boxes, straighten the shoes, rearrange the two flaps of white paper in each box, even to put a pair of laces to match in every one. But his father would not let him do this.

He kept looking about him, brightly at first, then more and more dully. It was a great treat to him when he found a calendar that was many months behindhand. He brought it up to date, tearing off each day separately and carefully, and putting the papers in a heap on the floor, ready to be taken away.

His father had taken off his outdoor coat, and put on a very old, shabby office coat, the lining of which showed at the elbows; and now sat in his sloping chair, looking at the stove. Sometimes he put a hand on the desk, and drew papers towards himself in a hesitating way; then he pushed them back, as if he were not certain what to do with them. After a while, he roused himself.

'Would you like to run an errand, Jont?' he muttered, so low that his son scarcely heard him.

'Yes,' said the boy, jumping up joyfully as soon as the meaning of the words came to him. He felt that he had been shut in the office for many hours, though in reality it was not much past ten o'clock.

'Take the umbrella, if it's still raining,' said his father, now definitely drawing some papers towards himself, and writing a note very quickly.

'Oh, *no*, father,' said Jont, putting on his cap and his short, shabby raincoat, 'it'll have stopped raining by now. I won't need the umbrella.'

His father was not listening, but was busy putting his note into an envelope and licking down the flap.

The boy's spirits rose at the thought of getting outside, of seeing the interesting sights in the streets, of once more being among people. He seemed to have been shut in some forgotten tomb with his father for a long time.

As he went down the steps into the street, closing the clumsy-looking wooden door carefully behind him, he almost bumped into a sharp-featured boy of his own age, dressed in a suit of very shiny serge and carrying a large parcel.

'Hello,' said the boy, 'are you t'new lad 'ere?'

'Ye-es,' said Jont, looking at him without smiling. 'Why?'

'Nay, I only wanted to knaw. I knew t'last lad.' They fell into step. 'You've got a funny cove for t'boss,' he went on. 'Puts Wholesale on 'is door, and sells boots retail to anybody 'at comes in t'back way for 'em.'

Jont thought over this. 'How do you know?' he asked with curiosity.

' 'Ow do I know?' Because I've 'ad some,' answered the lad. 'These is a pair.' He kicked up his right foot, almost overbalancing as he did so.

Jont walked on at his side, wondering whether to offer to help the lad with his parcel. He said in a mild voice, 'It's my father.'

'Aw,' said the other. They walked on for a while without speaking. 'Which way are you going?' he asked at last.

Jont found that he did not want to tell the lad his destination. At random, he said, 'Canal Road'.

'If I 'adn't this parcel, I'd come wi' you.'

Jont was glad because of the parcel. At a corner they parted without saying goodbye. The boy called after him, 'What's your name?'

'My name's Jonathan Gresham. What's yours?'

'Mind yer own business,' said the lad rudely. And for some time afterwards, Jont was tormented every time he put his head outside the door by the words 'My name is Jonathan Gresham,' repeated in a mincing voice by some person in hiding.

He went on with a dragging step, pondering over the answer he ought to have returned to the sharp-faced boy. The rain was still falling finely on to his face. He began to think of an invention, an umbrella which should be clamped on the head, with an upturned rim from which the rainwater would pour every time you bowed.

He half-pulled the letter from the pocket to look once more at the address. On the back, in his father's handwriting, were the words, Mr Goldstone, Gower Buildings, Maud Street. He knew that Maud Street was a short thoroughfare between two of the main squares of the town, where there were grim, high buildings filled with small offices.

The office of Mr Goldstone was on the very top floor. The boy climbed up a spiral stone staircase, listening to the noisy echo, 'shisha, shish' made by his feet. Behind doors fitted with ground glass panels, he saw figures moving like black shadows, or heard the sound of a quick-driven typewriter. Occasionally a voice or a laugh cut into the silence.

As he neared the top, the stairway narrowed. He raised his eyes, and saw above him a queue of people waiting; some holding the banister rail, some leaning against the wall; all sinister and quiet, watching his approach with dull eyes. There was something hopeless about their lounging figures. The boy's small, erect shape, his school cap, even his bare knees seemed to interest them in a morbid way. They were all waiting outside the last door, on which was written in thick black letters, 'I. Goldstone, Money on Loan'.

The boy, in his turn, stared at them with large, innocent eyes. Each one had a red book in his hand, and one or two were clinking coins together, very quietly. He wished that his father had not sent him to this place. What connection could there be between his father and a money-lender? Was he taking a receipt for some shoes that Mr Goldstone had bought retail?

He made his way steadily forward, through the queue of people, saying, 'Please,' in a gentle voice, or 'Excuse me'. Some made way for him willingly, some apathetically, but all in silence. He opened the door at the top. Inside was a small cubicle, where a man in a thin grey coat and bowler hat was leaning forward, writing figures with a short pencil on a piece of brown paper. Behind the small counter a dark, fat man was sitting at a low desk. This man looked up with a frown as the door opened.

'What do you want?' he said, in an unpleasant voice.

The boy was frightened, and because of his fear his heart began to beat quickly, and he felt short of breath.

'Please,' he said, 'I've brought a letter from Gresham & Co.'

'Oh,' said the man, staring at him, 'go wait at the end of the queue.'

The boy did not seem to understand him. 'I've brought this from my father,' he said, struggling to get the envelope out of his pocket. 'Mr Gresham's sent me from the office.' He wished the dark man to know he was businesslike.

'Is that so?' said the dark man, his voice still more unpleasant. 'Do as I tell you. Go stand at the end of the queue. Take your turn.' And all the time the man in the thin coat went on writing with his stumpy pencil.

The boy felt behind him for the door knob with his free hand. His eyes became covered with a film. He felt as if somebody was strangling him, pressing a thumb on his throat, just where he was wanting to swallow. He wished that he could be struck dead so that he would not have to move any more.

Slowly he pulled open the door, went down a few steps, and stood, his head bowed, his back to the others, looking through a small staircase window at the rain-wet wall opposite, trying not to think about the envelope in his hand, which he now knew contained no receipt, no money, but only some kind of excuse.

After he had stood for a while, he lifted his head and began to whistle, at first hesitantly but then with more confidence, a song he had learned at school; the sound that came from his lips was quiet, but as pure as a bird's song.

> 'Twas on the morn of sweet Mayday
> When nature painted all things gay,
> Taught birds to sing and lambs to play . . .

And presently it seemed that a ripple of hope passed through the waiting company, and took away a little of the heaviness from it. Nobody told him to be quiet, so the boy went on whistling his tune, moving upward step by step.

No Luggage?

AN OLD man, so thin that a hollow showed between his shoulder-blades even through his thick tweed coat, was sharpening a pencil on to a carpet. He had pale lips, and a beard, and eyes of an intense blue colour, sharp and eager still, though he was in his eightieth year. He had stood up, pushing back the wooden chair in which he usually sat, with its small, hard, torn cushion, so that he could attend better to his work. The pencil had a soft lead, and in spite of his care the end kept dropping off. Yet he stuck patiently to his task.

His wife, some years his junior, was drying stockings on a short, thick clothes-horse near the fire. She kept looking at her husband contemptuously, and at last she said in a harsh voice: 'Does it never occur to you to sharpen your pencil into the hearth?'

A frown appeared on the old man's brittle-looking forehead. After a moment or two he moved forward to the fire, folded the clothes-horse, pushed it to one side and continued his work. His wife looked at him in speechless fury, pounced forward, reopened the clothes-horse, pressing it against the thin legs of her husband in their round, neglected trousers, and then burst out in a spent voice: 'Haven't you any sense at all?'

The old man gave her a look like a goaded animal, moved back to his chair, spread a dirty, stained handkerchief on his knee, and went on sharpening his pencil into it.

'Why didn't you do that at first?' asked his wife, more mildly. Now that she had gained her victory, she was busily turning the stockings. They were almost ready to be taken and hung over the kitchen cord.

'Because it 'ud have been wrong if I had,' said the old man drily.

He began to think of the time, fifty years ago, when his wife had been a meek, timid girl, looking up at him with doves' eyes; hanging on his manly words; obeying him without question, yes, knowing no will but his. Now she hated him so much that she could

scarcely bear to be in the same room with him. This hatred of hers
kept them both alive, alert and interested, and was, besides, a great
joke for their children, who always inquired after it. 'Hallo,
mother. Haven't you pushed the old man downstairs yet? Hallo,
father. Where's that poison you've bought for mother?'

'Nay,' the old man would answer, smiling and shaking his head.
'I love your mother.' And so he did.

The children, all married, could not keep away from the old
house, especially the younger ones with their little children, so that
the place hardly belonged to the old people. One son, recently back
from Canada with his wife and two little boys, was living in part of
the house. The mother grumbled about this, too, though she could
not help feeling a sort of happiness when the boys pushed past her,
intent on some play, shouting and laughing. 'Get out of the way,
gran-maw, we're a train.'

She glanced out of the window, and said with a kind of mock
sigh: 'Oh, Lord, here's Molly and Frank turning up. Just at
tea-time, as usual.'

The old man stood up, a look of pleased surprise crossing his
face. The handkerchief full of pencil parings fell from his knee on to
the rug, but he did not notice it. Slowly and carefully he put up his
penknife and returned it to his pocket; then putting his pencil down
on the table, he went to open the door to his daughter and son-in-
law.

'Hallo, father,' said his daughter, pulling the old man forward
by his thin white hair, and kissing him tenderly on the cheek.
'Where are the kids?' She had listened for a second and had not
heard any noise. On the bottom step of the staircase was an orange,
a sixpenny flute, and a pair of broken slippers.

'Youngsters!' she called. She did not like to open the door that
led into the living-room of her brother, his wife, and their children.

The two boys came running out, shouting 'Auntie Molly' as
loud as they could.

Her husband and her father went back into the other room, and
she kneeled down, looking proudly and happily at her nephews.
Yet she only said: 'Who left all this mess on the steps? You don't
want grandma to fall and break her neck do you?'

'Yes,' said the younger one, giving her a mischievous glance.
Then he put his hands behind his back and shuffled through the

door. The elder sat on the step, blowing into the flute, which was broken and made no noise, peering sideways at this strange aunt, and thinking about her. She pushed past him and went upstairs to take her hat and coat off. When she came down again, the things were still lying at the bottom of the steps, but the black flute was wet and sticky.

In her parents' room, Frank, her husband, was sitting on a grey hassock looking down at the floor. Her mother had put a cloth on the table, and was setting cups and saucers, bending down to get them from a cupboard in the chiffonier. The old man was feeling in his pockets for his stump of pencil.

'Have you seen my pencil, mamma?' he asked. 'I thought I'd left it on the table.'

'Well, pick it up from the table if you left it there,' said his wife triumphantly. She had been waiting for this moment, having caused the pencil to fall to the floor by sweeping the cloth across the table top. 'How are you, Molly?'

'I'm all right. Don't *tease* him, mother. Here's your pencil, father.' She stooped and picked it up from the rug, together with his handkerchief. 'Can I help with tea? I don't want to, but . . .'

'Yes, you can,' her mother answered, pretending to be severe, yet breaking into smiles because she was fond of Molly. 'You can cut some bread, and butter it. Or, better still, make some toast.'

'Is this all we're going to get?' asked Molly, looking with dismay at a jar of jam and a fruit pie. 'I wish we'd stayed at home, we'd have had a far better meal there.'

'I wish you had,' said her mother, smiling and patting her daughter's smooth cheek. The old woman looked very pretty with her silvery-white hair and warm pink skin. She was a different woman now that somebody else was in the room. Another daughter, Isabel, walked in and began greeting everybody. 'It's just started raining, and I've got my best hat on. Can you lend me an umbrella to get home, mother? No, I won't stay.'

Isabel always made some excuse for coming, yet she always stayed. After a little persuasion, she took off her coat, and threw it over the couch head. 'I'll just have a cup of tea,' she said. They all knew that when the meal was ready she would eat the most.

The old man had begun talking to his son-in-law almost as soon as he had entered the room. The words came tumbling from him so quickly that sometimes they got mixed, yet he did not like anybody to help him out.

'Just do that Einstein th-thing on the rug again, will you?' he asked Frank. 'I've got something on my mind. There's a small point —'

Frank was always ready to explain the theory of relativity with apples, oranges, a lemon for the sun, and his tobacco pouch for the earth. If there was not a lemon for the sun and an orange had to be used, the old man would become confused, and seemed to be looking for the lemon under the table or even across by the door. Luckily, there was a lemon today, but at times, when Frank was not looking at it, the old woman would pass and push it into another position with her foot, and then pretend she had done it accidentally. Frank and his father-in-law knelt down, staring at their fruit.

'Now, this is the earth, and this is the sun — no, we'll have the sun a little more to the right. Move it up, father. Here we are. What is it you want to know?'

But when the old man saw the universe set out on the rug, his question had slipped him, or had answered itself, and he only said: 'Never mind, never mind,' and leaned forward on his hands, looking at the lemon with an obstinate gaze, as if he could make it yield up some secret. His wife kept saying derisively: 'Look at the silly old man!'

'Oh, come on now, don't be rude, mother. You've got visitors. Let's have something to eat. Get up, Frank. Do you think I spend my evenings ironing your trousers for this? Let's put the moon and stars back in the fruit-dish.'

Molly was moving about energetically, pulling chairs up to the table, pushing the two men away from what she called their little game. She had an extraordinarily quick mind, and had grasped the whole thing the first time it was put before her; but it had no interest for her except that it made her admire herself and her quickness still more. She felt sorry for the old man and the small points that he was so anxious to have cleared up, and had forgotten.

'What's the use of bothering your head about the universe and things like that?' she asked, passing her father a cup of tea. '*You'll* never find anything out about it. When you're alive, you're alive, and when you're dead, you're dead, and that's all there is to it.'

A sudden silence fell on the room, then the old man poured some tea into his saucer and drank it noisily. A brooding look had dulled his eager eyes. The clock seemed to tick: 'Eighty, eighty,' pushing him nearer to the gulf every minute.

Molly became aware of her cruelty. 'What have I done?' she thought, paling. She could never think of her father as an old man, and, of course, he was getting on. There was only one way to steer him away from his dread.

'Cheer up, father,' she cried, waving a piece of bread and butter at him. 'We all want to come to your hundredth birthday party. You've a long life in front of you yet. And will you never learn to drink out of your cup?' she said, altering her voice as if she were reprimanding one of the children. 'You —'

'When I was a boy, it was considered polite to drink from the saucer,' said her father. 'And to honour your father and mother —'

'What's the use?' asked Molly. 'When it only leads you to have daughters like me and Isabel. You might just as well have drunk out of your cup and kicked your father and mother to death.'

The old man had forgotten his sudden sorrow, and was talking again to his son-in-law. 'What's this fourth dimension, Frank?'

Frank was the sort of man who is expected to know everything. If you gave him a little while in which to think, he could always return a good answer. He played for time. 'Well, it just depends upon what sense you mean it,' he said.

But they had a good discussion while the women cleared the table, and went into the kitchen to wash up. The old man was fond of his son-in-law, and admired his round, brown eyes, his eagerness, the knowledge which welled up continually from some hidden store, and, above all, the youth and warmth which fairly glowed about him. In some strange way the house appeared to be dominated by women, and the old man seemed to be baffled by their strange, wearisome demands. He loved them, yet they hung about him like a swarm of wasps. 'Father, you're sitting on my best scarf. How mean of you! Now I'll have to wash it to get the creases out.' Or, 'That's my fruit-knife you're cleaning your pipe with.' Or, when he was smoking Empire-grown tobacco for cheapness and patriotism: 'What a stink! If you must smoke garbage, go into the garden to do it!'

He liked to sit with Frank, and let this woman-talk buzz harmlessly above his head for once. Time was slipping away so quickly, and there was so much he wanted to discuss.

The old man's thirst for knowledge only amused the others. Even Molly, with her quick brain, could not understand it.

'What do you think you are going to find out, father, with all this bothering of your head?' she would say. 'There's nothing to discover in your old Riddle of the Universe. All there is to know's been found out; if there's any secret to be revealed, it won't be revealed to *you*.'

'A-ah!' the old man would say triumphantly, looking up at her out of his keen blue eyes and wagging his forefinger. 'It *might* be! That's just what you don't know. That's just what nobody knows. It *might* be revealed to me.' And he would sit back, beaming at everybody with a sort of pride.

And the women would look at each other, and say derisively: 'Rambling again,' which was part of a joke they all knew.

When everything was cleared and put away, and the quiet Isabel had taken an umbrella and gone home, the two couples, the old and the young, sat around the fire. The old man was arguing, his eyes flashed, his hands thumped on the arms of his wooden chair; he even stamped his foot on the floor to give more emphasis to his remarks. Then his excitement made him cough, loud, harsh coughs, which shook his thin body like a storm.

During a paroxysm, Molly looked across at her husband and frowned. 'Cards,' she whispered, hiding her mouth from her father. The old man was very fond of a game of whist, but for some reason would never accept the suggestion from the women. He knew they did not like to hear the absorbing discussions which took place between Frank and himself, and this was one of the means he used of getting back at his wife's tyranny.

'What do you say to a game of whist, father?' Frank asked. 'Isn't it about time we got a bit of revenge. They beat us last time, didn't they?'

'So they did,' answered her father, wiping his eyes on his soiled handkerchief and then looking up joyfully.

Three of them liked whist, but Molly only played to please the others. She could not be trusted. When it was her turn to deal, she always contrived to shuffle an ace to the bottom of the pack. If they remembered this, or if one of them saw her do it, she would say: 'Well, you know I like to play this way. I always lose if I don't!' It seemed such a small point to her. She would only play fairly if luck was with her, or when somebody else dealt the cards.

This night Frank dealt, and luck was not with Molly. She was glad when the door of the room opened, and the two little boys put their heads round.

'Come here,' said Molly. 'What's that you've got?'

'I've been drawing something,' said the elder one. 'A double-decker bus, full of people.'

He had drawn the bus, the driver, the starting handle, all complete.

'You're a little marvel,' said Molly. 'Now draw me a ship.'

The little boy looked at her, and calmly decided that he would not draw a ship or anything else. He wriggled away from her detaining arms, and went back to his brother, who was standing near the door, looking as stout as a robin in his red jersey. 'Jackie wants to tear another piece off the wallpaper,' he said, looking solemnly across at his grandmother.

'Tell him I'll tear another piece off Jackie, if he does,' said the old woman, fingering her cards uneasily.

The little boys went racing away to see their father, who had just come home, and was having something to eat. And soon afterwards they came back, clad in short, triangular nightdresses, to say good-night. They never minded going to bed, but would play and talk upstairs, and have shouting games, until somebody had to go upstairs to quiet them.

Molly kept yawning, and hoping that her brother and sister-in-law would soon come into the room. She wanted to transfer her cards, which were getting worse and worse, to her brother, and read.

After a little while, they came. The sister-in-law was smiling. 'What do you think?' she said. 'I put that little beggar's braces on the mantelshelf in the bedroom, and I told him they were there so that everybody who went upstairs could give him a smack with them, if he was noisy. And he said, "Put them on the bed, mother, they'll be handier." What can you do with a kid like that?'

All the same, she spoke with pride, folding the middle part of the evening paper carefully as she did so, that she might read the Births, Marriages, and Deaths column in greater comfort.

Molly gave up her place and picked up a book that was lying on the couch. 'What's this, about Freud?' she asked. 'If it isn't the limit, father and Freud! What do you want to know about him?' She held the book high above her head.

The old man, who seemed to have one eye on his cards, one on his daughter, and a frown between them, said: 'Well, I've learned plenty of new things in that book. It's given me a lot to think about.'

'I'll bet it has,' said his daughter feelingly. But she had only heard about Freud, and had never read anything. She kept looking in the book, skipping several pages. Once or twice she became interested. She kept ejaculating: 'Oh, yes, he's right in some things. Right enough,' and pulling at her lip with a finger and thumb. 'He's got one of my little habits here,' she cried, smiling across at her husband. 'But I like it, and I'm not going to give it up.' Yet from that place, she treated the book with more respect. When she had skipped through it, she said calmly: 'But I know all this. There's no need to make a book about it.'

'Think about the other poor, unenlightened people in the world,' said the old man sarcastically. He began to tremble. 'You think you know,' he said. 'You think you know everything. You know nothing!'

'Now, father,' said the son from Canada, in a soothing voice, 'it's cards at the moment, not philosophy.' And he patted the old man on the back gently, feeling the sharp shoulder-blades moving under the thick coat.

'You're all alike,' said the old man. 'There's so much to find out, and so little time to find it out in. I want to know. I want to know about everything. Everything in this world and in every other world,' he finished passionately. The cards in his hand were almost falling from his grasp, and he was making feeble attempts to straighten them. Everybody was silent. He regained his composure, and went on playing with an effort. But in the end he and Frank won; and with the growing interest his face became quietly radiant.

'We'll show them how to play whist,' he kept saying, as he drank the coffee that Molly had just made for them all. 'We'll show you.' He seemed as if he could talk about nothing now except the cards; how this game was played, and that one; what he had held in this hand, and not held. There was not a sound from upstairs. The boys were asleep. It was getting late.

Molly sat silent, thinking of how much she loved her mother, her father, the torn, yellowish rug which had been bought from a neighbour who had gone to America twenty years ago; the chiming clock which had been mended, and now said: 'Oo-cuck, oo-cuck,' instead of 'Cuckoo,' every time it struck; the little boys upstairs in bed in the room where she used to sleep; the high draughty windows which rattled when the wind blew; all these people gathered in this warm room.

Her thoughts went as far as they could go, and she became filled with contentment. 'There's been sorrow and happiness. There'll be sorrow and happiness again — all of the same kind.' She was quite convinced that there was nothing more to know.

She believed that it was not good for the old man to argue and become upset late at night, so while he was still talking about the hands they had held at cards, she said abruptly: 'Let's go, Frank.'

When the two had their outdoor things on, and a light had been lit to show them down the path, she kissed her mother and said good-night. The old man followed them to the door, where a chill from the cold earth seemed to meet them. He looked, in some indefinable way, like his elder grandchild, appeared as small and shrinking when his daughter put her arm about his frail shoulders and kissed him. 'Good-night', he said in a very gentle voice. He waited in the cold until they had waved to him from the garden gate. The light behind his head seemed to make a flickering halo of his thin white hair, and to outline his whole figure. Then he shut the door.

They walked along in silence for a time. The gravel of the road was slightly wet, and clung unpleasantly to their shoes. There was a mist, no higher than the lamp-posts, moving gently in currents of air; it was now cold, now almost warm. The lights looked dim, the sky above them pitch-black.

Molly began to think about her father. In a kind of vision, she seemed to see the old man packing a suitcase — a suitcase already full to bursting; trying to cram into it more things and still more, so that it could accompany him on some journey he must make. And yet she could not help feeling that he would not be allowed to take it with him.

The Wife

I WOKE up at ten minutes past seven, but went off to sleep again, as the alarm bell does not ring until half-past. During the second or two in which my eyes had been open, I had noticed that the morning was sunny, that a breeze was moving the top half of the grey-blue curtains, and that the many-coloured eiderdown had slipped off me and was entirely on Kay's side of the bed. I was too sleepy to move it back, and in any case, I was not cold.

At half-past seven the bell rang. I always keep the clock on a chair at my side of the bed, so that I can thrust out my still tired hand and push the switch over to silent. I did this, then I began to tap my foot against my husband's, and say, 'Get up! Get up!' He did not move, so I pushed my hand against his side. In a little while he said, 'All right', and opened his eyes and smiled. Thus the day began.

We had agreed to halve the labour of lighting a fire. 'You shall take out the ashes, and bring in the coal and wood, and I will light the fire.' This was the theory, but for a fortnight I had had a cold, so every morning Kay had lit the fire, and I had stayed in bed for ten extra minutes. As soon as he was out of bed, I rolled over on to my left side, sliding my knees up until they reached my chin. I kept so for a minute or two, then began to kick about in the pleasant emptiness of the bed, stretching and yawning. My eyes stayed open for longer and longer periods. I felt that I should like to jump out of bed, so I leapt out quickly. If I waited, and began to imagine that I had jumped out, I knew it would be much harder in reality.

We have a table, but we do not use it for breakfast. After the fire is lit, and Kay is shaving, I get a meal ready for him. He likes two slices of brown toast, with an egg on the top of one, and some bacon on the top of the other. I put this down on a plate on a chair, and his cup of tea on the mantelshelf, which is not too high; and he comes in and eats his breakfast. He sits in a light brown leather chair, with a velveteen cushion in it, from which tiny feathers are always coming out, and eats his meal from off the other chair. This is always a source of satisfaction to us. We think of the millions of people who are eating their breakfasts from tables; but we are much more comfortable this way, sitting up to the fire. I take only a drink of tea, as I do not like to have my breakfast with my husband. I had rather run about after him, getting him salt and pepper, filling his cup again, or fetching him some biscuits from the cupboard if he has not had enough to eat.

When the newspaper has come, we read snatches from it. I love my husband, and he loves me. If I stare at him too deeply when he is eating, he looks angry and uncomfortable, and he says, 'Don't watch every bite I eat'. Then I look away. When he stares at me for long minutes, I, too feel uncomfortable. I think he has found some flaw in me which attracts and repels. I feel myself become a caricature under his eyes. Yet it is not so. We are just marvelling in the secret satisfaction each feels for the other. We have grown so much alike in the years of our marriage that people take us for brother and sister.

After Kay had eaten his breakfast, he went into the greenhouse to look at his plants. There are very few of them, and they are covered with a perfect plague of greenfly. The other day he put some of his plants under a box and fumigated them. Now they are covered with blackening insects; but all the same, I see some new green ones are creeping about, trying to avoid the bodies of their brothers. He has wonderful ideas about having a greenhouse full of flowers. Perhaps they will bloom, perhaps not, but it has pleased him putting the seeds in and planting out tiny green shoots in pots. Last year he was very proud of one, which he called by a long foreign name. He put it in a pot by itself, and tended it very carefully. But when it was grown, and he was waiting expectantly for it to flower, he touched it accidentally with the back of his hand, and it stung him, because it was a nettle. All the same, it looked very beautiful, pale green and haughty; and he had the satisfaction of looking at it every day for a long time, and being proud of it.

When he had been in the greenhouse, it was time for him to go. One of his bootlaces broke. I feel pleased when things like that happen, as I always keep a secret stock of bootlaces, and studs, and small things like that he might ask for; lemons, or fuse-wire, or grease for the wheelbarrow. It is worth the bother of remembering the small things to see the frown disappear from his brow when I bring out what he is asking for. He asks guiltily, apologetically, 'Have we about four yards of flex?' and I am so delighted to be able to produce it from somewhere.

But what does this matter? He put the bootlace in his boot, threw his yesterday's handkerchief on the floor, asked for two more, and after kissing me twice, and looking excitedly at a new flower which had just appeared in the garden, he went. The flower was a polyanthus. He came back for his pipe, which he had left on the mantelpiece. We looked at each other kindly, and he went. Friday is the day he goes to London, and it is a long way to go — two hundred miles.

After he had gone, the woman brought the milk. She has had a goodish walk, and it is lonely, so we like to have a chat. She tells me of any new marriage, birth, or death, and I tell her what I think about them. She likes to go to dances, but she is very tall indeed, and that makes me wonder how she goes on about partners. It seems to me that they will touch in the wrong places. But perhaps I am wrong. I have never been to a dance.

I dread Fridays — this one more than any of the others. It is not wise to think of all that might happen. Here I am, with the wireless to listen to, and a gramophone; a piano to play if I want, also a Hawaiian guitar. We have a lot of silly little things, like tin whistles and imitation saxophones, which are very lively things to have at a party. Most of our parties are composed of members of the family, so that we do not have to be polite to each other, but can speak the truth. If things are slow, Gee will yawn and say, 'What a rotten party,' several times, missing all the t's out of the words, which makes it sound funny, and not so true.

My brother Gee is very clever in some ways. He can imitate people and things, and when he is inspired, he can make one forget life and death for a little time. He can be a camel for a few seconds, chewing disdainfully, looking down at us as we stare madly and helplessly at him. And he can go down some steps behind the couch where there are no steps, carrying a pile of boxes, turn round and come back up with perfect seriousness. This almost makes us believe in immortality, I do not know why.

Sometimes my husband gets a cold, which he thinks is influenza. When this happens, he ties a large brown scarf round his head, takes three tablets of aspirin, and goes to bed. He looks at me very reproachfully every time I go into the room, as if he wanted me to know that he is gravely ill. But he will not let me send for the doctor. He says, 'No, no. Give me a day or two and it will go.' This is because he is afraid of all doctors. We are never really ill. I had rather read than go out and buy a lot of food, so that we do not get too much to eat.

But what use are we in the world? It is very hard to find out. Kay is always trying to invent things. He thinks he would like to make cinema films stereoscopic, and he has made a large machine with lenses and cardboard flaps and big tubes on it; but the contraption refuses to make films stereoscopic. Kay wants to stay alive for ever, so he finds difficult things to think about. He has theories about the harmonics of light and heat. And he is always taking things apart and putting them together again, so that he need not think that the end of his life is slowly approaching.

How time drags, this Friday. When I catch sight of myself in the mirror over the mantel, lines seem to be growing deeply between my nose and my mouth. I cannot smile. I can only look at myself severely, like a school teacher in front of a refractory class, and find nothing good in my face. Why do I care so much for my husband, and think that he might be far away, and hurt, and wanting me? I have other interests, but how much better they are when he is near me!

Yes, when we are near each other, things are different. If I think of anything funny, I can call to him and tell him. He comes out of the garden in his dirty boots, dropping lumps of earth from under them, and I shout at him, 'Clodhopper, filthy brute!' and he makes a face at me, or pushes me calmly out of his way if I become too obstreperous. I know he has come in because he wants a screw-driver just that minute, and instead of asking me to get it, thinks he will fetch it himself and save me the trouble. He forgets altogether about the dirt dropping off his boots; and I am glad, because I would not like him to be the sort of man who thought of every little thing like that.

We live in our little house, away from streets and people. We have placed our affections on each other, and each is terrified lest its own load of love should vanish into that blackness which presses around it on every side.

Yes, I love my husband, and he loves me. But for all that, we quarrel sometimes, especially when we are on a bus. Then I say, 'Fool!' quietly and bitterly, because I know it hurts him to be called a fool; and he says, 'Aye, well, you mind your own business,' more loudly than he should; and I feel humiliated, and look out of the window. By and by I see something which interests me, and I forget our quarrel, and point it out, but he says, 'I'm not interested,' in an indifferent voice; and I feel as if somebody has poured lukewarm water on the back of my head. Yet I notice he looks out furtively. We have been trying not to look at each other, and it is easy, as we are sitting side by side; one can turn one way, and one the other. As soon as our eyes meet, we are done for, and we laugh at each other. At those times, even as I laugh, I feel that it would be pleasant to chop his hand off with a sharp axe.

What would happen if he died? Each time he is late, I think about this, so that sometimes when I hear his footsteps on the path and his hand turning the door-knob, I have to tear myself out of a deep, dark dream, where I can see him lying in bed, with his feet looking very large and stiff under a cold white sheet, his hands resting one below the other on his stomach, and a white handkerchief tied under his chin and round his head, as if he were suffering from some ghostly toothache.

There would be two thousand pounds, and the furniture, and me. I should be knocked to pieces, pounded with heavy blows, undertaker's blows, parson's blows, even funeral tea blows. I do not know about these things, but they would happen. Yet for seven minutes today I forgot him utterly. This is how it happened. I was reading a poem about a snake which came to drink at a water trough. I was also eating chocolate with almonds and raisins in it. When I started the poetry and the chocolate, I was thinking, 'Why am I reading about this snake? It is nothing to me. Let the time be here when the eight-thirty-two train comes rolling up the platform side, stops, and Kay gets out of it and comes hurrying, frowning, eagerly looking for me, his ticket held so that the collector can take it quickly; fatigued, smelling of smoke, as he has done so many times before (spare him now!). But the snake took hold of me, and before I knew it I was in Sicily, and the chocolate tasted sweet in my mouth. The next time I looked at the clock, seven minutes had passed utterly without thought of him.

Is this how it would be? The tears, the horror, the blank silence;
then perhaps one day poetry, food, and a little forgetfulness. After
that, more and more forgetfulness, less silence. I should keep his
photograph deep down in some forgotten box. For a few weeks I
should certainly pray, and imagine that he answered me, and be
comforted; but dustily, without truth. I should not like to die,
because I like the sensation of swinging my legs, both together, out
of bed every morning, and feeling my toes press into the hair of the
rug.

Of course, some day I shall die. But I do not believe that.

I had very little breakfast, so at noon I was hungry, and warmed
up something I had made yesterday in a pan. It was onions and
potatoes and milk all mixed together. I ate it out of a basin with a
spoon which I had bought at Woolworth's. I have six good spoons,
but I did not want them to taste of onions.

I wonder what love is? I think about my husband for a long time
together, as if he were a lot of eggs in a nest, and I the mother bird.
And when he comes home, other days, and looks round the door,
with the evening paper in his hand, his eyes are shining, and he
says in a whisper, 'I've been thinking about you all day long!' Now
I know when he says this that he is a liar, because a business man
does not think of a woman all day long. But it heartens me. I know
that he has been conscious of me, and that I am necessary to his
happiness.

Yet I have been thinking of him in a different way. I ought to
have been working for his comfort; instead, I have been wondering
if there might be an eternity for us, so that we might fly about
together, laughing slyly at the angel we don't like, or helping those
that have got into difficulties; and it has taken me so long that I
have done nothing else. There are crumbs on the hearthrug, and
only things out of a tin to eat. Yet we are happy together beyond the
dreams of heaven, in spite of rates and taxes, and tinned beans, and
promises that we make to other people and forget to keep.

Now he is in London, in those great, roaring streets, where
everything moves so quickly, and the words all sound different, so
that one is confused. *He* will not be confused. He is quick, and light,
and careful. Last night I put a patch on his drawers. I am not good
at sewing, and my patches make him laugh. I just do them to
amuse him. Yet I had to put the patch on, for fear that he should be

in some accident and people might say, 'Who is this man with torn drawers?'

Why should my husband have to go away to get money so that we can live? When we are parted, it is like tasting death drop by drop. If only all goes well, and he comes back to me, dirty, tired, smelling of tobacco smoke — how happy we shall be, until next Friday, when this will happen all over again.

The Man in Black

THE end carriage of the train waggled like the tail of a duck. There was no guard's van. At Wennington, or some station like it, another train would probably be hooked on to the back. There were plenty of empty carriages, and it was a slow train, but I got into this one partly because of its unusualness, and partly because of the man in black.

This man would be between fifty and sixty years of age. He had the long face, long upper lip, rounded head and fanatic eyes of a certain type of Yorkshireman. But instead of sitting in pride he had the appearance of a man whose back has been broken and who does not yet know it. With the shaking of the train he too shook on the hot red cushions, his yellowing hands, with their uneven, bluish nails, clasped over his knees.

The journey was going to take three and a half hours. The train would stop at every sun-steeped station of the seventy miles. It was the slow which followed the express as a sort of compensation. I sat on the opposite side of the carriage, in the far corner, looking at my companion; idle, with clasped hands, my book on the seat at my side. I marked his thinning grey hair, the little curled veins on his brow, the wrinkles about his eyes, and the two deep lines from nose to chin.

'It's a grand day,' I said reflectively.

'Aye,' he replied, after some time.

It was curiously warm and airless. A fly alternately buzzed and crawled upon the glass-framed views of flat, grey, and almost impossibly beautiful places. As I dozed this noise, and the sound of the softly clacking wheels made me think I heard a muttering voice which went on and on and on. Words fell on me like drops of fine rain.

'Her name was Elizabeth Ann, and we called her that. None of your Bettys and Bessies. We'd been courting for two years when he came. Harry Mitchell, his name was, and she never looked at me after that. He had a big brown moustache, and he sang bass in the choir. I never was a hairy one, and I couldn't sing; but it wasn't that. Of course she went for a walk or two with me, Sunday nights, looking back over her shoulder. And sure enough, he'd come along and she'd walk slower and slower, till he'd catch us up, and we'd all three walk together. It wasn't long before they left me out.

'I did all I could, but it wasn't much. I made things unpleasant for a while, as anybody young would do. I'd thought to be married within a year or two. I'd saved up, not a lot, but I was saving, and she'd made one or two things herself. But it wasn't long before they were married. He had a bit of a farm, you see, and I was only a labourer then.

'I began to hate them both at the wedding and all because they looked at one another in church. I went out and walked to Twentyclough, fancying I shouldn't sleep that night. It was over thirty miles away, but my Aunt Jinnie lived there then. I waked her up at four o'clock in the morning, and she called me all the names she could lay her tongue to, but I only said: "Give us some breakfast, Aunt Jinnie"; and she did. She'd thought my mother must have dropped down dead or summat, and in a way she was disappointed. And then I walked back.'

We had stopped in our desultory journey at some small station. I opened my eyes and gazed at the man in black. He sat quite silent, staring at his clasped hands. Nobody troubled us. The train, for some reason, stood high from the platform, and I could see the sky and a few clouds, and the hill and moor tops. As soon as the train started the monotonous voice began again, mingling with the doodadoo, doodadoo of the wheels.

'Harry Mitchell couldn't do owt wrong when he got Elizabeth Ann. His beasts were best for miles around. Nought ever ailed 'em. Everything went like clockwork, and I didn't like to see it, so I went over to Twentyclough and lodged with Aunt Jinnie, and got myself a better job. And for a few years I just stayed there, hating Elizabeth Ann and Harry Mitchell. I thought if she'd married me things would have gone different with me. I might have been happy if ever she'd looked at me the way she looked at him. But in the end I had to go back. My mother died, and left me her bits of things. I kept the house on; she only rented it, but we'd always lived there, and I took a job with Harry Mitchell. I wanted to be where I could see him, and her too. He laughed a bit and said: "Let's see, didn't I do you out of a lass?" And I laughed, and I said: "Not that I remember." He didn't think I was worth bothering about.

'There's plenty of hard, mucky work on a farm. You're up early and you bed late, but I didn't mind that, because I'd got something for my hate to work on. The pleasure I got out of that was a hundred times better than the pleasure I'd ever had out of a kiss, which was as much as ever she'd given me. It's true I liked jobs near the house best, where I could see Elizabeth Ann out of the corner of my eye when she went about the yard. She'd altered a good bit in five years, and she didn't look at Harry Mitchell in quite the same way now. I began to fancy it was me she was looking at. I was younger than him, and I had five years more on me than when we were at our courting. She had wavy hair, light-brown coloured, and sometimes she'd stand at the window, combing it. She fancied that wavy hair, and she'd hum some song, holding the pins between her teeth, and I'd look at her once, maybe, but not again. And in a bit the song 'ud stop, and I'd hear her walk away vexed. After a while she was generally to be found somewhere near me, whether I was in the yard, or the byre, or away over Long Pasture.

'This went on for a long time, but I had patience. She began to fret, and to talk sharp to Harry Mitchell in front of me. Before long he was over at Tebcroft drinking every night. And she would ask me into the kitchen, and sit sewing and looking at me in the lamplight. And sometimes she'd pass me so that her apron or even her hand would touch my knee. But I just sat there like a wooden image, biding my time. And before long it came.

'Harry Mitchell kicked a dog a bit too hard when he'd had a drink or two. It needed a hiding, but not that way. There was a lot of to-do, and an inspector came over, and one thing and another, and before he knew it, he was in prison at Tebcroft. When they took him I promised to see the farm all right. "I'll look after everything for you," I promised. Elizabeth Ann was standing by me, trembling and crying. I looked as grim as I could, but I wanted to laugh. "My hate's coming to something, after all," I thought to myself.

'We drove home together, side by side on the board across the milk float. And she began to laugh as soon as we were out of the town, trying to talk soft to me. I never looked at her. She put her hands over mine on the reins and leaned over and put her face against my cheek, but I pushed her away and went on driving. And when she came pestering me in the barn when I was looking round after supper to see that all was safe for the night, I kicked the lamp over in a way that I knew, to make the light go out, because I couldn't bear to look her in the face. How I hated her!'

The train was crawling across a high common, bare and greenish-brown under the sun, but I seemed to be in the barn, too, smelling the smoking candle-wick and the hay, hearing the click of a fallen rake and the rustle of a fieldmouse; in a black, close space, where there was hate, and then no sound but the rushing of blood past ears that could hear nothing.

'After that she used to try to make me stay, but I always hurried to get away. I'd started courting again, but there was no thought of marrying in my head this time. It was a young girl called Martha, fair and delicate, and I knew as soon as I clapped eyes on her that a year would see her in her grave. I was a few weeks wrong, but she served my purpose. I hung round her, courting every night as soon as my work was over, and acting as if I never saw another woman. Elizabeth Ann tried to make me feel jealous. She would be making up to any man who'd speak to her, and many a time she was seen in the evenings wandering up and down the lanes restlessly. It doesn't give a woman a good name at any time, especially when her husband's in prison.

'Harry Mitchell was nearly due to come out before she came moaning to me and told me she was going to have a baby. "I wasn't sure for a long time, and now its further on than I thought."

' "Harry will be pleased," I said.

'She called me a fool, and asked me if I thought he was one, too. "He'll know it's not his, he'll know, he'll know," she kept on saying. Then she began making up to me and asking me to take her away.

' "Where should I take you to, and why?" I asked. "You know I've no money if I'd wanted to take you anywhere, which I don't. You should ha' thought of that when you chucked me for Harry Mitchell."

'She began to cry and say she didn't know, and that I was a

brute, and I just kept on looking at her and hating her, knowing all the time that she'd never tell on me. And neither did she. A day or two before Harry was due out, and I was away taking a load of muck for a gentleman's garden, she let herself tumble downstairs to rid herself of what she'd gotten for her pains. She was in bed for a month before she died. You see, she'd been left lying at the bottom of the steps for hours and hours; she'd made a mess of herself all right. I took a long time over my ride, whistling till my cheeks were sore, for I can whistle if I can't sing.

'And when Harry got home he'd stand by her bedside and shout at her: "Tell me who it is, you arrant bitch." Many a time I heard him. And he never once thought of me. Men never see what's just under their noses. "You've looked well after the beasts," he would say to me, "but I wish you'd thought to keep an eye on yon she-devil. I've heard about her traipsing the lanes at all hours." She never asked for me and I never wanted to see her. I helped Harry to bury her and we hushed up everything as well as we could. And sometimes I'd go with Harry to Tebcroft, and drink with him if he paid; and he'd get telling me how fond he'd been of Elizabeth Ann, and what he'd do if ever he found the man that ruined her. I'd take his arm and help him home.

'Horses are queer things. I mean race-horses. I got to doing a little betting in the pubs on the sly. I was no punter. I did a bit of bookyin'. I took 'em, and I hit lucky. It seemed as if nothing could go wrong with me, now. Harry kept on backing 'em, and nothing 'ud go right for him. Well, it went on, and in the end I got the farm.

'I told you Harry was older nor me. I wanted to keep my eye on him, so I gave him the job I'd had. It was a long walk for him to the cottage, so I built him a sort of wooden hut near the barn, and let him live in that. Many a Saturday night he came walking in, weeping drunk, trying to get upstairs into one of the bedrooms — there were four in the farm — but I never let him stay. I'd never slept under the same roof as him and I wasn't going to begin it. He'd say it was cold in his hut, and damp and lonely, and that the rats got in and wouldn't leave his things alone. Well, I knew it was damp and cold and lonely, my hate had built it that way. I'd stand at my window many a time, rubbing my hands and being glad that the wind was making his chimney smoke again.

'Sometimes I'd hear him singing and shouting to himself, and

I'd go downstairs just to say: "Less of that, Mitchell" — I called him Mitchell now — and to see the way he was going. Lord, he was a smart man when he first came sauntering down the lane after me and Elizabeth Ann. And now his big moustache was streaked with grey and running loose over his lips. He'd gone all rheumatic, his eyes watered half the time, you wouldn't know him for the same man.

'But it's all over now, all over. I went down one morning and he said he couldn't get up, he felt bad. This was just over a week ago. There'd been a lot of rain, you know. But I made him get up and come out into the rain with me. "I don't feel bad," I told him. "If I can work, you can." And I kept him on outside jobs all the time. But for all that, I was too soft. I fetched the doctor after three days. The doctor said he ought to be in the house, but I said: "It's my house. This is where he lives." No man can make me do what I don't want. Yes, Harry Mitchell died in the hut I built for him to die in.'

The air was fresher, clearer. It seemed as if the first sea breezes were entering the carriage, although we were still some miles from the coast. The man in black sat looking straight before him — grim, hostile, lost in some memory or other. At the same time he had the appearance of an empty shell.

I asked him where he was going. Twice I had to ask him before he heard. Then he said: 'I've a fancy to see the sea.'

The Apprentice

ONE warm spring morning a good-looking plumber's assistant of about nineteen came swinging out of a doorway, carrying a porcelain water-closet on his shoulder, and whistling 'My love's an arbutus'.

He gave a glance up at the bright blue sky, at the sun in the south-east, and thought with rapture of the evening that was coming, when he would see the young girl, Pattie Lancaster, with whom he had fallen in love. She had promised to meet him, to walk with him. Where could they go? Down Leeds Road, up Apperley Lane, across the fields? No. People would always be passing, and he felt that he wanted to sit down and look at Pattie Lancaster for hours, without any interruption.

Perhaps she would let him hold her hand. He trembled at the idea. Other fellows thought nothing of putting their arms completely round a girl's waist, kissing her, and having their faces slapped soundly for their trouble. But he wasn't that sort of a man, nor was Pattie Lancaster that sort of a girl. She was a star dropped straight from the sky into the grey city. Her hair was yellow, her eyes blue and kind. There was something about her that made him feel as if the whole world was his to conquer. He grasped his burden and trod firmly on the flagged pavement — bing, bang, bing, bang.

His working clothes of blue drill had been washed many times, and shone in all the places where the material was double and the hot iron had gone over it. A small torn place at the knee had curled over on itself. The blue stuff suited him, making his healthy pink face appear even more young than it was. He had dark hair, hidden by a grey cap with a peak pulled to one side and downwards.

Where should they go? The day seemed to be rushing onwards like a dream, and he had not yet thought of a place. Of course, it would be splendid just to walk along the streets with Pattie Lancaster, to look down, adoring her; but there would be more people still — people in desperate, tearing, senseless hurry and scurry, pushing against them. If a man so much as grazed Pattie with his elbow — he grew tense at the thought, his whistling ceased, and an expression of extreme anger crossed his face — 'I'd knock him flying,' he said aloud, staring straight in front of him. A meek little man about to pass him stepped off the pavement into the road, accelerating his pace. The young plumber laughed.

There was Wood Lane, of course. Now that the new road had been made, people had deserted Wood Lane. That wasn't too far. And somewhere near the top, before you got to the newly built houses, there was a gate leading to an old, unused stone quarry. He had been up there several years ago, looking for mushrooms. Two or three tall black trees, which carried only a few green leaves at their extreme tips, had somehow been left standing at the bleak quarry edge. You could see all the town from there — that is, if you wanted to look at the town. It might be interesting for Pattie. She could look at the distant view, and he could look at her.

He smiled ecstatically. How was it possible that everything had changed in such a short time? All the people seemed to have altered in some subtle way. Last week he had lived a different life, had had different ambitions. Wherever his thoughts ranged now, they always came back to settle round the head of Pattie Lancaster.

'I love her!' he thought. But he would not dare to tell her so for years. Would she ever love him? Was she, at this moment, dreaming as he was, walking through the spring morning on air?

He was nearing the river, that dark, town river which ran full and sluggishly under the stone bridge. Today, he thought, he ought to be walking along the banks of a pleasant country stream with his beautiful Pattie. They should be going hand in hand into some flower-filled future. They should . . .

His burden was slipping a little, so the young man rested on the bridge and began to transfer it from his right shoulder to his left. Beneath him the light sparkled on the filthy water, making beauty even of the scum.

As he stood there, he looked with sudden interest and apprehension up the road beyond. A young girl was walking down, swinging a market-basket. She had a blue and white dress on, blue stockings, and low-heeled shoes. He saw that it was Pattie Lancaster.

She was coming straight towards him, not yet looking his way.

There was nothing he could do, no place in which he could hide the hideous water-closet. He looked about him, but there was only the blue sky, the bare stone bridge, and the river beneath him. He blushed with shame. Pattie Lancaster and this? No, never. He pushed the ghastly white object, which ten minutes ago had seemed only a part of his daily work, into the river. It made a great noise as it hit the water.

The girl looked up and put her hand to her hat-brim. Coming towards her was the young man she liked so much, and with whom she was going out this very evening. Why had her mother made her take this old basket for the vegetables; and why had she put her most childish shoes on? She felt as if she could have sunk through the ground. Didn't he look handsome in his blue drills? As frail as a curl of smoke, the thought passed through her mind that some day she might have his clothes to wash.

'Good morning, Leslie,' she said shyly.

'Good morning.'

He raised his cap awkwardly, seeming to lift his head with it, and they stood looking at each other.

'Did you hear a splash?' she asked. 'I thought I did. I thought perhaps a dog had fallen in the river, or something.'

She was only saying this to make conversation, and wished that she had mentioned the sunshine or the warm air instead.

'No, I didn't,' he answered her politely.

They kept looking at each other and saying they must go. The young man scraped the toe of his boot aimlessly round and round a flaw in the stone paving, and the girl played with a piece of loose straw from the handle of her basket.

'Mother's waiting for some potatoes,' she said apologetically. 'I must be off.'

Yet they did not part, but kept on smiling at each other.

'You won't forget. Tonight at six o'clock?' he said hoarsely, and then blushed at the sound of his own voice.

'I won't forget.'

He turned and began strolling at her side towards the shop in silence.

'Oh, don't come with me,' she admonished him. 'You must go back. Remember, you're working. I only stay at home and help mother.'

The young man went back to the bridge reluctantly, turning every now and then to watch Pattie Lancaster in her blue and white dress and low-heeled shoes. He felt light and free, as if he were absorbing the air and the warmth, and even new life. But when he reached the middle of the bridge he suddenly clapped both hands to his head, and looked with horror over the parapet at the swiftly running river. Then he stood without moving for a long time.

The girl went forward to buy her potatoes, her eyes sparkling, her lips parting in smiles that she could not control. She kept saying under her breath: 'Oh, the poor boy! Whatever will they do to him for that?' For, of course, she had seen him long before he had seen her.

She looked back over her shoulder and saw him standing on the bridge, forlorn. Beneath her laughter a pang of pity shot suddenly through her heart, and, at that minute, she began to love him.

Spring Day at Slater's End

PEOPLE still take their Sunday walk up the hill to Slater's End, though much of the view is now obscured by the bright new houses which will in their turn grow mellow, crumble, and help to form fresh dust for the quiet green grass to cover. But you can walk higher than any houses have yet gone, climb over a lumpy stone wall, and find yourself on a wild moor, where the sheep shun you and curlews cry; and if you are strong-willed and ready to walk in steep places, you will come quickly to the Nab; and over the Nab — on the wild side, not the sheltered one — is the small, walled cemetery known as Slater's End.

Only the very oldest folk are buried there now. For the road is bad, and they have to be 'walked'; but if they say 'Slater's End', it has to be Slater's End, these old women who still wear their bonnets to chapel, and these old men who are sure of eternal salvation for themselves and eternal damnation for most other people. If they have been harsh to their children and driven them away; if they have oftenest got 'rayther the better side of a bargain'; if they have pinched and saved, and denied themselves and theirs pleasure, Heaven is open to them. They have, at any rate, kept away from the sins of the flesh. Yet long ago, the young were carried here too.

One spring morning — not a Sunday, so they were alone on the road — an old, old man and his granddaughter were walking up the hill. They peered with interest into the gardens of the new bungalows, admiring the neat rows of daffodils, always late in this cold part of the country, which lined the straight, cemented paths.

The little girl had a round, rosy face, direct, wondering brown eyes, and comical little tufts and tails of brown hair which straggled over her cheek. Each time they got in front of her eyes she would say, 'Oh, dear!' and push them back under her hat. But the puffs of wind, which came apparently from nowhere, always dislodged them again. And at length she would cry out, in imitation of some admired elder, 'Grandpa, just look at my ridiculous hair!'

The old man walked at an even pace, tapping the ground every now and then with his stout cherrywood stick. He was glad of the pale, warm sunlight, and of the song of half a dozen larks which grew now louder, now fainter. His eyes and ears and legs were good yet, he thought thankfully. The hair was off the middle of his head; he had a tonsure, surely the most becoming way for a man to lose his hair. If there was some at the front, where you could see it yourself, and some at the back, where other folk could see it, what more could you want?

He had the long face, with its long upper lip, and the tight, grim mouth of the moorland folk. The colour of his eyes was almost washed away, but it had been palest blue, even in his youth. He was dressed in the black suit which he had had for over thirty years, and for overcoat wore a sort of black frock-coat, with two buttons at the back. In the flap of this he carried a spotted red and yellow handkerchief, on which he liked to blow his nose with a loud, challenging sound.

He was of the old breed, yet time had subtly softened him. There was the Post Office, where he drew not only his old-age pension, but also a pension due to the death of an unmarried son in the Army. There were the 'pictures', to which everybody, including his independent daughter, Marion Alice, went. These he resisted with a cunning 'Nay'. And there was the wireless, which even his authority could not keep out of the house. For this he had a secret fondness, but would pretend that he did not care for it when other people were in.

Up the road went the two. Sometimes the little girl took hold of her grandfather's hand, sometimes she ran from his side to pick a flower or a piece of grass; and sometimes they rested for a while, leaning against a wall, both staring dreamily at the opposite hill, which seemed to be lying with its head at rest against the bosom of the cloudless sky. Then off they would go again.

In one garden there was a row of washing hanging on a line, swaying gently. A woman in a white apron and a blue mob-cap came out of a door carrying a creaking basket filled with wet, folded white sheets and towels. She smiled and called out, 'A lovely morning, isn't it?' The child stared back at her, unsmiling, while her grandfather answered solemnly, 'It is, indeed,' and went tapping his way upwards.

When they came to the wall, he climbed over it with stiff legs, and the child threw her roundedness forward and scrambled over. 'Are we going right to the top?' she asked, and went running forward without waiting for an answer. She had seen a lamb, separated from its mother. It was afraid of her, and did not know which way to turn, so it opened its mouth wide and bleated. Silently, with bobbing motion, the old sheep approached, looking at the child with a mixture of menace and fear. She stopped, gazed at the sheep with wide eyes, and ran back to the old man, shouting, 'Grandpa, hide me, hide me quick!' When she looked out from the flap of his coat there was nothing to be seen; the sheep and the lamb were hidden behind a rock. And for a long time she walked quietly.

'Where are we going?' she kept asking. Or, 'Grandfather, what's that?' as they saw a hare, quite near. The old man was absorbed in his thoughts, and did not answer. 'I know. I know; it's a rabbit,' she answered herself. 'A rabbit, a rabbit, hurray, a rabbit!' She jumped over the tufts of hard, rough grass on to the bright green pieces which had been nibbled close, finding a hundred things of interest. She picked up a broken bottle, and for a long time carried a piece of the bluish glass carefully before she tired of it and threw it away.

She ran up to the old man, patting his leg above the knee with her chubby hands. 'Is it far, Grandpa? Is it far to the top?'

'Not so far, now,' he said, 'and then we'll have a rest.' He felt in his pocket, slowly. There was the sound of the crackling of a paper bag, and with difficulty he brought out of it a piece of toffee, which he gave to his little granddaughter, who stood near him with sparkling, expectant eyes, and eager mouth half open. She pushed the toffee into the side of her mouth, and sucked noisily and contentedly.

The way grew steeper, and their walk slower. The morning was perfect. Far below, the busy towns, linked together by twisting white roads, shimmered in the mist of their own smoke, and gave out a faint, faint hum, punctuated by occasional louder noises, such as a hammering clatter in the railway yards, or the sound of a bell chiming the quarter-hour.

They came very suddenly on the top of the hill. There was a

triangular platform, sheltered by a large rock twice the height of a man and three times the length of one. It was grassy, but cropped almost to the dust by the sheep. The little girl flung herself down and rolled about like a puppy, and the old man sat on a knoll, resting his chin on cupped hands, his elbows on his knees, his cherrywood stick beside him on the ground.

When the child tired of rolling about, she crept close to her grandfather, picked up the walking-stick, and after having smelt its sweetness until she could sniff no longer, walked about in imitation of the old man, pulling down her mouth severely, tapping often with the stick, and all the time darting bright glances at him from the corners of her eyes.

Although his eyes followed her for a while, his thoughts were in the past. Sixty years it was, or more, since Lily had died. And here he was, up at Slater's End, not many yards from where her bones were lying, remembering not the life which had come between, but that short year when he had known Lily.

He could see her face now as he saw it then. Pale, with just a little colour in her cheeks when the wind put it there. Her hair had been flaxen when she was a baby, she had told him, but it had grown a deep golden brown with the years. She had grey-green eyes with tiny pupils, a large nose, and a pretty, crooked mouth. She had small ears, pressed close to her head, and dressed her hair to show them. She was very thin, so thin that when he thought about her slightness his heart contracted with pain.

She was seventeen when he first saw her. She had known trouble and responsibility already, and these had drawn grave shadows across her face; but as she met him, a beautiful smile had come over her like sunshine, and driven those shadows away.

They had not a great deal to say to each other when first they met, boy and girl in the spinning-mill; and they had plenty of work to do. Yet on every pretext, the boy was down at her end of the room, just to see that she was still all right.

It was a long time, almost six months, before he dare ask her if she would go with him for a walk. 'I don't know,' she had said, in her shy way, 'I'll see.' And he waited for a long time one day, until at last she came.

'I thought you'd have gone,' she told him, breathlessly, when she saw him standing in the shadow of a high wall at the bottom of the mill-master's garden. 'I'd have come before, but I couldn't get out.'

'That's all right,' he said, gruffly. And his heart was crying, 'I'd have waited for you for ever, you beautiful little dove.'

'How d'you like it at the mill, then?'

They strolled along, that first time, talking mainly about their work, and about a little man at the mill called Edgar, who was henpecked, and always getting into trouble. She grew animated, and laughed at her companion's jokes.

'I didn't know you could be funny as well as kind,' she said. And they wondered what the stars really were, and why the moon looked just like it did. And they were silent for a long time, thinking vague thoughts; walking a little apart, happy to be with each other.

They met again and again, but she could not walk so far as on the first night. 'I don't know how it is,' she said. 'I've never felt like this before. I used to be as strong as strong when I was a little 'un.'

One Sunday they arranged to get up early and walk to Slater's End. 'It's grand up there,' he told her, 'with the larks and all. You can see for miles around. Let's hope it won't rain!'

The morning had been perfect, just as this one was. 'We've got to get down in time for me to cook dinner,' she said. That was why they had gone so early. And there were no buses then to carry them half-way up the hill. She had on her best frock of dark green, with a white frill at the neck and wrists. And she had on a little green velvet bonnet. He could see the knot of hair in her neck just as plainly now as he did that day.

She let him take her hand to help her up. Her eyelids were strangely heavy, and not even the touch of the wind put colour in her cheeks. 'I don't know why I'm so tired,' she kept saying. But it did not occur to either of them to forgo the excursion. It had been planned, so it must be carried out.

Up the road they walked. There were no houses there yet, only fields reclaimed from the moorland. The lane became a path, which dwindled away to the merest track. 'I will get to the top,' Lily said, gritting her teeth in determination. When they came to the wall she sat down. 'Let's wait a bit,' she said. 'We've time yet.'

Just such another blue sky, he remembered, with the opposite hill resting its smooth cheek against the sky as it was today. He had put his arm about her shoulders. 'Lily,' he had said, looking down at her. 'Lily.' And then he kissed her.

They had almost raced up to the top of the hill. They laughed and teased one another, and rested breathless on the ridge at the top of the hill. 'Isn't it — ? Isn't it — ?' They couldn't find a word to say of what they thought about it all. He could hardly look at the distant view, when here was Lily, near him. He wanted to kiss her again. Clumsily he pressed towards her. 'Lily, lass?' he questioned.

But as the boy looked towards her, terror came over him. She had leaned forward, her eyes were closed, and bright blood was trickling from the side of her mouth.

'Lily!' he called. 'Open your eyes. What's the matter, lass?' But she continued leaning forward slowly, so that she would have fallen but for the pull of his hand; and the blood ran on her white collar and down her neck as if it were seeking some hiding-place.

His trembling hand tried to brush it away, but more came. So he gathered her up in his arms and set off down the hill, falling over the hummocks, cursing them, cursing the larks which sang so loud and maddeningly round him, cursing the bright, blind sunshine, and the lonely hill-side. And presently she was in her house; and after that, she was dead, and he took some flowers to lie near her, and climbed the hill to Slater's End again.

And quite soon, while he was still a boy, he married Maggie Halliday, and now, here he was, his little granddaughter beside him, the years fled away like seeds of grass in the wind. There were his sons and daughters down in the valley, with their sons and daughters; and up here, the old man sat with his dream.

The little girl had tired of the rest, and run away. She had found her way to the rusty gate of the walled graveyard, and was looking through it with interested eyes. She still clutched the cherrywood walking-stick in her hands. The old man's voice came to her from far away, 'Come along, Becky, come along home to dinner.'

> Home to dinner, home to dinner,
>   There's the bell, there's the bell.
> Pudding and potatoes, pudding and potatoes,
>   Ding, dong, dell. Ding, dong, dell.

she sang, and ran to take hold of her grandfather's hand.

Five for Silver

A WOMAN stood on the pavement in Oxford Street one Saturday afternoon in March, waiting to ask a policeman something. She carried a baby about a year old in her arms — a boy, very fair, with serious blue eyes and long, white fingers. The child was dressed in a blue woollen coat and bonnet. He was small for his age, and looked rather like a dignified old man masquerading. Now and again, replying to some intent, passing glance, he would give a wide, toothless smile, and then relapse once more into apparent thought. His mother waited patiently, both arms clasped about him in an ungainly way. A brown waterproof bag was hanging from her left wrist.

'Can you tell me a nice bus ride, please? But don't send me to Richmond. I've been there four times.'

She spoke with a north-country accent. As soon as the words got into his brain properly the policeman smiled, pulled a bus guide out of his pocket, and murmured to himself: 'Twenty-five, twenty-six.' 'Would you like the East End, do you think?' he asked, bending to hear what she would say next, ready to catch the words quickly.

'Oh, yes, please,' she said in an eager, grateful way.

'Well, walk down to that crossing. You see where those buses are coming round that corner . . .'

Yes, she saw them, like a great fleet of red galleons bending with the wind and waves, like gorgeous, dressed-up women walking down the steps at the end of a pantomime, like covered wagons dashing across a film prairie. You knew there were only so many, yet they came and came, giving the illusion of something never-ending.

He pointed. 'They come from Victoria Station. They go through the City and the East End. It's a long ride.'

'I've got three hours,' she said anxiously, breathlessly. 'Baby's just been fed, and he wants to go to sleep.'

That did not interest the policeman. He was busy reckoning the times for her. 'You'll do it nicely,' he said. 'Twenty-six is the longer ride.'

'Thank you very much,' she said. The policeman went on giving her directions. She heard him say 'Bond Street' once or twice, but her mind was repeating: 'The City, the East End'.

The bus was covered, and she climbed to the top when a traffic signal shone red, and sat in the front seat of all, putting down her bag and shifting the child on her knee so that he could see out of the window. But he was tired and closed his heavy eyelids. Again she moved him until both were comfortable.

There was intermittent sun and cloud. People shuffled aimlessly along beneath her and the moving traffic raced like splashes of mercury along a board, stopping and staring, it seemed, with no reason.

Her gloves were in the bag beside her. She found it easier and warmer to carry the boy without gloves. There was no wedding-ring on her left hand. Many a time she had been going to buy one for herself, at Woolworth's; or even a gold one, when she had plenty of money. But it was only in shamed seconds that she thought of this.

What hurt most now was that she knew she had made a mistake. The boy's father was not all she had taken him to be — a hero, a god on earth. He was simply a skunk. A skunk who slunk. She laughed, but there was no one else in the bus to hear. It was not a pretty laugh. There was nobody in the bus downstairs either, but the conductor kept calling out the names of streets from force of habit, or for practice, and she heard his voice as if it were a roll of tape, coming upstairs, unwinding itself.

For months, even after he had kept away as soon as he heard her news, she had forgiven him, loved him as passionately as ever, had been infatuated with his memory. His child was to be the most remarkable child — she looked down at the sleeping baby and was pleased with his calm perfection, the regularity of his features, the nobility of his face serene in sleep — a most remarkable child (bound in strong corsets, unloosed with groaning at night, as soon as she had fought that last steep bit of road. 'You are getting wide, Freda.' 'Yes, I know!' She couldn't keep the blush back; but of course nobody could suspect Freda Crowley, never did. 'I eat far too much.' She used to say it frankly, sincerely, smiling.).

But that was at home, in the north. And sometimes she stole out, those rain-wet or wind-filled nights of winter, smelling the hidden spring. No corsets then, but a woollen vest wrapped longways. 'I'm taking you for a walk, baby,' she would whisper. And quite foolishly she would go along the road to the edge of the moor where they had been together, alone for the first time.

It was high and quiet, with only the green brow of the hill above. There was a gentle slope into the pastured valley. The night was dark, and very silent, yet they had difficulty in hearing each other's whispered words. She had seduced him urgently, suddenly. He had been angry, and called her vile names. 'What are we to do?' she asked. 'Men don't run after women any longer. And I wanted you.'

He had driven the car back like a madman. A small boy, coming home from the cinema, ran across the road in front.

'Get out of the way, you devil,' he shouted. 'I'll murder you!'

She had felt a little contempt then, but the waves of her emotion had not quite receded, were not to recede for a long time. She was too physically happy. She turned and saw his unhappy face. 'Don't.' Her voice broke. 'Nothing's any different. We're just the same as we were.' He was willing to believe her. He turned towards her, taking his left hand from the wheel, putting it over both of hers, which looked so inert and were so alive (she was without gloves then, too, and the feel of his heavy driving glove made every nerve respond), and murmured something to her which she heard as in a dream through the heavy noise of the car. It was even darker here, on the New Road, than at the moor edge. She strained to see him, the wide eyes she loved, the pale cheeks, the curled mouth with its one-sided smile.

'Now you'll hate me.'

'I'll never hate you.'

Their hands freed mutually, and for a second or two she put hers to her eyes, until she heard him say, 'Don't', in pleading.

For months afterwards she had not seen him alone. When people were there they looked at each other with restless, broken looks, pouring out short, polite speeches like thimblefuls of brandy.

The second time, he came wanting her against his will. It was early summer. There were smells of cut wet grass and crushed fruit blossom. She would not think of that night. For of course it was night. His for her was not the kind of love that would face the morning light. She could hardly believe that she was in his arms again. He was almost afraid of her quiet calmness. . . . 'And I love somebody else; you know that.'

Yes, she knew that; but underneath, even then, the thought occurred: 'It's a poor kind of love. And to say it now, here with me. He must get a horrible kind of pleasure, saying it. And afterwards, with her, he'll remember me. What'll he say then?'

But she could not help abasing herself before him, saying the words which built up a new picture for himself to himself. He was like an archangel to her, an archangel and a skunk mixed. Not because he had gone away, but because he had gone denying his child in his mind, brushing it out of his mind, forgetting.

She had told him in smiling happiness, expecting nothing.

'Oh, my God!' he said, in terror. 'Can't you do anything?'

'Do anything?' she asked, perplexed. 'What do you mean?'

'To stop it,' he said. She noticed sweat on his forehead. 'What do you think I mean?'

'But I don't want to stop it.'

'If that's how you feel, there's nothing more to be said, is there?'

She saw escape in his eye, and wondered whether to torture him; then decided not. 'I'm going away before long,' she said mildly.

'Look here' (he said 'Look here' quite a lot), 'you won't do anything rash, will you?'

'I won't kill myself for you if that's what you mean,' she said ironically.

He breathed his relief.

'Goodbye. You might tell me one thing before you go.'

She waited for him to say 'What is it?' but he remained silent.

'Have you ever had one loving thought of me?' she asked frankly.

'No,' he answered.

So she turned and walked away to hide the blinding tears of self-pity that came tumbling out of her eyes. He did not follow her.

'Stop it, you fool,' she advised herself, finding her handkerchief with a competent hand.

After the night walks, tied up in the woollen vest, it was harder to squeeze into those gripping corsets in the morning. She must work, must save money for those few weeks when she would be unable to work. She kept typing bright articles for newspapers on the portable typewriter Uncle Dick had bought for her in the palmy days when he came over from America, quite rich, but not as rich as he pretended to be. For some reason she was able to sell all she wrote, and the idea came to her that she might be able to live in London when her child was born.

Quite early, before the baby had begun to show, she mentioned the idea at home and among her friends and acquaintances. She exaggerated the amount of money she got. With what she would make and what she had saved, she was bound to live. And she had lived.

The bus was now in Holborn. Still there was nobody in it but herself. It felt like a chariot and she like a queen riding it. Memories of Boadicea, she thought idly. It was in Holborn that she had made her first friends. She had been carrying the boy in her arms. He was tiny and delicate, and she would not leave him to another woman's care. She saw a bookshop with the sign BOOKS in blue or green sticking glassily out over the door.

She went in, and there was a bookseller, a big man dressed in blue trousers and a blue shirt with a steel fastener, looking like Jesus, but quarrelling with somebody quietly. She half backed out, but the man said 'Come in. It's all right, we've finished.' He said. 'This is my wife. We were just having a row.'

He threw some books from a bench to the floor, and she sat down. quite silent, looking at the bookseller's wife and smiling. Presently she stood up and talked to the wife, whose name was Ruth, and the big man nursed the baby and looked after his customers too.

A man asked, 'This yours, Karel?' and he answered 'No' with an effort, as if he should have been the father of all children. She kept thinking 'I ought to go now,' so she said, 'I can't buy any books. I've got to live on my wits. This baby's mine and I'm not married. But I'm glad to have met you.'

'You come up and spend the day with us on Sunday,' the wife said in her soft, hesitant voice. The bookshop became a kindly cave. On Sunday she enjoyed herself, expanding in warm friendliness. She sat in a cool garden under pale sunshine, and watched the bookseller's children, the blue-eyed, dark-haired one who talked so seriously to a little boy on the other side of the hedge, and the hazel-eyed baby, who wore corduroy trousers and tumbled over every stone on the path.

Before long she was telling Ruth about the child's father. 'It's curious, I despise him, but I still love him. I seem to be marking time just now, waiting for something to happen — waiting to understand why I've done this thing at all. Shall I wake up one day and think I am a sinner? I'm in a fog; I don't understand either faith or repentance.'

'The best thing to do is not to think about it at all,' said Ruth, still soft and gentle. 'Try to make your baby well and strong.' She took him indoors and gave him orange juice.

The City was very quiet, even for Saturday afternoon. The bus rocked and rolled through narrow streets with their vaguely familiar names. At last she was in the Mile End Road. Here was life and colour. The clouds had won against the sun, but fruit stalls cut the gloom, each orange a miniature sun in itself. There were apples and bananas, black and green grapes. Each fruit bloomed with a different lustre, appearing before her eyes, vanishing, and being replaced by a fresh showing.

And here a different people walked. She thought: 'He wouldn't like this road. He would keep away from it (denying it as he denied you, little bastard). He likes the conventional things, tea-parties, bridge (with a little cheating thrown in, seeing you're playing for money), Gilbert and Sullivan, my God, shaving cream, hair cut and nails clean, and shoes *never* down at heel; a chapter to finish off the day from a book about the wide-open spaces, or the sea (would he be sick? Would he? perhaps not). "I love somebody else, you know," *that* certainly means church every few Sundays.'

There were Hebrew signs everywhere — black, robust, like the people themselves. In high, injured tones a hoarding whimpered: 'If ye believe in Me, ye shall have everlasting life.' 'What a gift,' she murmured. A young couple came walking on, hand in hand, strangers, gazing at everything with wide eyes, then back at each other, smiling, loving. She smiled down at them, something melting in her heart, and thought: 'That's the first time I've been happy to see lovers for a long, long time.'

The baby slept as if he would never wake again. The bus filled gradually, perhaps because it had begun to rain slightly. The further away it rolled the busier places appeared to be. People were doing their weekend shopping. She was interested, at last, in every one.

As usual the fruit shops were the things she saw most. Calm, placid suburbs with people buying oranges — and every now and then a vile, gruesome murder somewhere. Size nine stockings, and that faint smell of powder on his coat-collar — strange, she hadn't minded it at the time. 'I love somebody else.' She was thinking of his first kiss. The top of a flight of steps with a wooden hand-rail. Quiet, with dusty sunlight falling gently through roof windows. A speck of that same dust might have been heard falling. She could not remember whether she had shut her eyes or not, but something inside her laughed in triumph at the hard, bitter touch of those heretofore only seen lips. Of course, there is always a first kiss and a last.

The end of the journey came and the baby waked. His face was flushed and drunken with sleep. He stared out of the window, still in his mother's lifted arms, blinking. A horse and van drove up among the houses marked Cloakroom (Who would want to get off here? she wondered), and the boy jumped, smiled, and made some unintelligible noise. A man in uniform came up, changed the sign, and told her that one of the standing buses went before his. 'But we only wait ten minutes; no need to get off.' So she stayed, talking to the child.

The rain came down more steadily now, and the bus filled once more. A woman in black sat next to her, staring out of the blurred window at nothing. She had two talkative children, a boy and a girl of about eight and ten, who stood up, breathing on the window and smearing their arms on it. The baby leaned forward and smiled into the woman's face, but she kept on looking out of the window and would not notice him. He said his small words to her, and touched her coat-sleeve lightly, but still she stared forward with the same glazed look. They passed a graveyard, the bus stopped, and the boy said in a high, piercing voice, 'My daddy's in there, he's *deaded*.'

So that was it. The woman's husband was dead. Had she loved him? — this tall, angular woman with these ugly, insensitive children. It was like something silly and sentimental in a cinema, the rain, the crowded bus, the boy's raucous voice, the subdued movement of people getting off unwillingly into the downpour.

And the last kiss. 'Freda,' he said it very gently, in surprise. 'I've never called you Freda before.' Neither had he, she had always noticed. But it came with such swift sweetness, he must have thought of her often. She was taken by surprise, and her lips were cold. She did not wish to disappoint him in anything. She thought of his footsteps on the pavement, the glowing light of his cigarette, the hesitation, so faint, so fine, so studied, before he came.

In the hospital where her child was born she had tried not to think of him at all. The nurses had been wonderfully kind. She would not allow his name to appear on the birth-certificate. 'Father unknown,' she had said in a hard voice. Nobody believed her.

She shrugged her shoulders. 'Think no more now, it's all over. Look at these houses, row on row.' But there was a night when baby was ill and began to cry with pain. She sat up in bed saying: 'Hush, darling!' trying to bring herself sufficiently from sleep to light the lamp. When it was lit, the baby still cried with the harsh passion of his pain. She rocked him in her arms, her foot slipping down the smooth sheet. The small, blue-enamelled clock on the table said four o'clock and she was afraid of something she had heard about life being at its lowest ebb at that hour.

He threw himself backward and screamed into the night that was filled with stupor, with remorse, with heavy sleep. She rubbed his little belly, 'Be quiet, my darling, my darling; we'll be sent out of the house, my little one, my own.' But the tears poured out of him, wetting his ears, his hair. She held him passionately, leaning over him, frightened, not knowing what to do. This had never happened to him before.

And she too, had cried, rocking him in her arms. She looked at the empty place in the bed, and thought: '*He* ought to be here. He ought to share this, too.' In a flash of agony she saw him lying, turned away from her, frowning in half-sleep. ('Can't you keep that baby quiet?' petulantly.) She grasped at the dream of complete life between two seconds of time. And when the child was quiet, she lay with him, exhausted, not even bothering to turn out the light, holding the dream like a scroll in her brain and not at all in her arms.

Once she had seen five magpies fly out of a wood. To herself she repeated:

> One for sorrow, two for joy,
> Three for a letter, four for a boy.
> Five for silver . . .

'Five for silver,' she thought. 'That's all I've had, not six for gold, nor seven for a secret.'

She was tired, now, and baby was jumping about restlessly, turning, even whimpering sometimes. People still hurried along, hidden under bobbing umbrellas. Rain streamed across the silver-black roads, and the sky hung greyly just above the bus stop. Again she was left alone to go through the deserted City. She began to think of her room with a certain amount of happiness. (Two changes yet, and rain. But people were kind.)

She got off and had a cup of tea in a Lyons shop that was almost empty. 'The world is quite nice today because I have a little money.' She caught sight of herself in a mirror, smiling, contented, ordinary. 'A little longer, and I shall be able to bluff even myself.' But she could not see beyond tomorrow or the next day. Baby would never grow up, she would never change; there would be nothing else definite. She had exhausted herself, tumbling out her treasures all at once like some creature that lays it eggs and dies.

On a table behind a screen she attended to the little one, making him comfortable for the last stages of the journey. 'How did I get here at all? What is there that I have to do?' she wondered, her hands mechanically smoothing and tying. But she had seen fruit in barrows; fruit that made her think of other countries, other worlds, people a little different, who made her think of other countries, too. There was a world forming where there had been darkness so long.

She sat the child up on the table, letting his fingers close round her own. They looked at each other patiently for a little while, then she sighed and said: 'I can't tell you, baby,' and withdrew one hand to feel in her purse for some coppers to pay for the tea.

Pin's Fee Wife

THE THREE sons of the fishmonger Gabitass were dark and queer, and nobody knew them at all well. The fishmonger had a shop in which were sold also hearth-brooms and gramophone records. He sold a good many records, because he always took a penny or two off the price. He would say: 'Well, one-and-three to you, but don't breathe a word of it.' The hearth-brooms were good ones, and hung from the roof in bunches of six.

When Mr Gabitass had been a widower for three weeks he went away and brought back with him what he called 'a young female' to do the housework and help in the shop. The girl, Effie Shepp, was little and fair, with skin and complexion like an early summer flower. She was an orphan, and had been ill-treated a good deal in her life, so that she was rather simple: easily frightened and easily propitiated.

She worked hard from morning to night, scrubbing floors, black-leading ranges, moving furniture about and cleaning behind it. Now and then she was allowed to serve in the shop, and learnt to clean fish. For some reason she liked this. She wore a little green jersey, with the sleeves rolled up, and she would cut up the fish very deftly, talking about it to the customer.

She had no pride, and would say, laughing out loud: 'I'm a servant, I am, and it's a grand place 'ere. My word, if you'd 'ad the life I've 'ad you'd think it was a grand place too. And these lovely records. Look! I can play 'em all day long if I like, when I've washed my 'ands. Mr Gabitass says I can. Can't I, Ronald?' she would call through into the kitchen.

Ronald was the youngest son. He had a long, spotty face and greasy black hair, but he impressed Effie because he used unusual words. He said he would like to be a munition in a ship, and she knew what he meant. He went out with the cart, and had spare time on his hands, so that he often talked to Effie. He would sit in the shop, putting on record after record, and chaffing with her.

Once he followed her up to her attic bedroom and tried to open the door, but she was shocked, and called out: 'Ee, you mustn't do that, Ronald. I'll tell Mr Gabitass.' And for a long time afterwards she was frightened, and followed the old man about the house like a forlorn kitten whenever Ronald was in.

Twice a week Ronald would clean himself up, and shave, and put on a white collar and a blue tie with paler blue silk crescents on it, and go to the pictures. He never asked Effie to go with him, and if he saw her outside would turn his head away stiffly. The first time she saw him out of doors she squealed, 'Ee, Ronald,' but he walked hurriedly past her. She was abashed, and thought, ' 'E *is* grand,' and she respected him much more, even when he smacked her behind rather hard as she passed him in the shop.

The other brothers, Bert and Mitchell, went out to work. Bert was a clerk in the office of a brick works, and Mitchell helped in a garage, and was engaged to the proprietor's daughter. These two were very distant with Effie, and hardly ever spoke to her, though she took her meals with the family. She called them Mr Bert and Mr Mitchell, because they were older than Ronald.

Bert was uneasily ashamed of Effie's presence in the house. He would mumble to his father, 'Can't she eat in the scullery?' But the old man, who had grown fond of the young girl, would not let her go into the scullery to live, as it was very damp and draughty. So she continued with them in the warm, gaslit kitchen, and when Bert brought his friends in he would say, 'Put the tea in the parlour,' without looking at her. Mitchell had his meals in the parlour, too, when his girl came to see him.

Effie could not find reason for this. 'What's up wi' them? Is there something the matter with their stomachs?' she would ask Ronald, who sat with her in easy familiarity, shirt-neck unbuttoned, legs sprawling over the couch-arm. Old Mr Gabitass would reply: 'Nothing wrong wi' their stomachs, lass, only summat up wi' their brainpans.' It was much more warm and comfortable in the kitchen than in any other room.

Effie was eighteen when the old man died. She was very much upset and cried a good deal, because he had been very kind to her. She helped with the funeral, though that was a niggardly affair. The three sons bargained with the undertaker before they would let him begin. He was a nice, quiet little man called Hackney, and he did not like the way they behaved, and he had never been used to that kind of thing. He took his trade with great seriousness, and could not bear any deviation from what he called the natural rules.

After the father's death, Mitchell married without telling his brother, collected his belongings and left. There was only a little money. That went to Mitchell, to help buy a share in the garage. The other boys were to have the shop between them. Never very friendly, they began to hate each other. Ronald could not see why Bert should go out to work and expect a share of the shop takings too. He would sit and grumble to Effie by the hour, and when he had finished he would put his arm about her absent-mindedly, and after a while she ceased to wriggle away from him.

But she was watchful and cautious as well as a little scared. She began to call Bert 'sir', and do little jobs to help him. Bert would not take any notice of her, except to tell her sternly one day that she must in future take her meals in the scullery. He had heard whispers of mild scandal about Effie and Ronald, and would have dismissed the young girl altogether except that he did not know of anybody else who would work as cheaply and as well.

Effie did not much mind living in the scullery, which was only as cold as the fish. She kept on trying to ingratiate herself with Bert, who remained adamant. When Bert was out Ronald would ask her into the kitchen and either talk to her very grandly or try to take her on his knee.

One night Bert walked in just as he had succeeded. Effie liked Ronald very much indeed, and of late her attempts at repulsing him had not been really strong. 'Why shouldn't I kiss him if I like him?' she had asked herself. So she kissed him very sweetly.

'What's all this, you dirty little slut?' Bert said. He did not shout, but there was a sneer in his voice.

Ronald looked at him with hatred. 'You get out o' here and mind your own business.'

'It is my business. I don't want our family mixing with scum.'

Effie had jumped up and stood looking at Bert, sniffing and biting her fishy hands. She had a red woollen frock on. Her hair had recently been washed. She looked like some pretty, timid child who was afraid of being struck.

All the rage that Ronald had felt for a long time came out. He had given up taking out the cart, and the shop profits were now considerably smaller. An idea of hurting his brother came into his head and stayed there.

'Don't call my young woman scum either,' he roared. 'Me and Effie's courting. Aren't we, Effie?'

'Y-yes,' whispered Effie.

'You're nothing of the sort,' said Bert, glaring at her angrily.

'All right, sir,' said Effie, beginning to cry.

Ronald banged on the couch-end and stood up. 'We are,' he shouted, 'And what's more, we're going to be married at Christmas. Aren't we, Effie.'

This was the first Effie had heard of it, but she dried her eyes and said 'Yes'.

'A fine time to hear of a thing like this when I've just lost my job!' said Bert.

The quarrel ended with supper. Bert had his in the parlour, the other two in the kitchen. Ronald was uproarious, and kept kissing the young girl loudly. He opened the communicating door so that Bert should hear him, but as often as he opened it Bert banged it shut. And Effie's face grew warmer and warmer, and a kind of frightened shame sprang up in her heart as Ronald kept on pawing her with his big fingers.

'Stop it, Ronald,' she begged him. 'It isn't right.'

'Course it is,' he boasted. 'We're going to be married.'

'Yes,' she said doubtfully, 'but "going to be" and "married" isn't the same thing.'

'You're a fool,' he said angrily. 'And I s'll stop bothering with you if you don't mind.'

Now that Bert was at home, Ronald began taking the cart out and regained some of his lost trade. The brothers kept quarrelling about the takings, and sometimes Effie tried to make peace between them. Bert would say, 'Shut up, you,' to her. He had bought some tools and was making a model of a church with all kinds of curious materials: corks, and hairpins, even pieces of chewed chewing-gum and tinsel scraps.

Ronald and Effie were married very quietly, and went to the seaside for their honeymoon of three days. It was extremely cold and foggy, and they stayed inside the lodging-house most of the time playing Ludo with the landlady's children. Effie enjoyed this, and would afterwards refer to the seaside as 'a lovely place', although she had scarcely been outside the house. She could quite believe that fish came from that miserable expanse of winter water, and looked at them with pity when she got back to the shop.

'Poor things,' she would say to the customers. 'Per'aps it's as well they're goin' to be warm for once in a nice 'ot pan.' She felt that now she was Mrs Gabitass she could talk even more to the people who came into the shop. She was perfectly happy, and sang as she went about her work. She loaded the cart for Ronald, fetched and carried for Bert, and on Wednesdays, the afternoon the shop was closed, cleaned in the house.

Ronald still shaved and dressed himself up twice a week and went to the pictures, but he never took Effie with him. He would not take her out at all, so she walked by herself the few minutes she had to spare, and if she passed him just stared at him and waited to see if he would speak. He never did.

Bert kept getting letters with the postmark 'Victoria, Vancouver', and when he had read them he would pass them across to Ronald. The two brothers had become friendly again, and often left the shop entirely to Effie, going out and not coming back until very late. The customers, who liked the child, would say: 'Aren't you ever lonely, Effie?' but she would reply: 'Ee, no; I've always lots to do.'

Ronald began to grow more and more like Bert. He now looked down on Effie and regretted his marriage very heartily.

'It's this way,' Bert would whisper to him. 'You can't take her about with you. You know you and me *are* somebody. We've got a shop, and we've a brother who's part-owner of a garage. We could mix with anybody, but just look at her . . .'

At that moment Effie was pulling the inside out of a fresh herring and saying, a little wistfully. 'I would like a baby'. She was talking to a woman who had a child in her arms. 'But Ronald says whatever should we do with a baby 'ere? There's too much to do. But, all the same, I should like a baby.'

'Just listen to her,' said Bert, nudging his brother and sniggering. 'What can you do with a blabmouth like that?'

Ronald grinned in a sickly way.

The letters from Vancouver kept on coming. They were from a Mrs Lonsdale, a cousin of their dead father. She had two daughters: one called Rita and the other Fay. She kept sending photographs of the girls. One of them was fat and one thin, and, judging by the snapshots, they always seemed to be dressed in light colours and enjoying themselves at a picnic. 'What a life!' thought the two young men. Yet they knew that their aunt kept a boarding-house and that things could not be always like this.

The boarding-house must have paid very well, for in one letter Mrs Lonsdale said that she was coming over, and would certainly stay with the boys for a week or two.

'I don't know how you are managing since your father passed away (Poor Man),' she wrote, 'but I think you need a Woman about the House. So we are All coming to see you. It will be in May, I think, or early June, just when everything looks so nice in the Old Country.'

'Now what shall we do?' said Bert, in dismay. They had not written of Ronald's marriage. 'Now what shall we do?'

They began to treat Effie more distantly than ever, and once more sent her to have her meals alone in the scullery. On Wednesday afternoon they sent her out for a long walk. 'Don't hurry back,' said Bert. So she went into the spring sunshine. It was a lovely day, there were young celandines down in the part where a little brook had overflowed its banks. All the trees were bursting into life, and the sky was light blue speckled with white clouds. The young wife went stamping along the road because she had been told to walk, wishing that she had someone to whom she could talk, or a baby to hold in her arms.

'It's been a nice change,' she said humbly to her husband when she entered the house once more. He was reading a green-backed paper, and did not answer her, only shuffled his feet. She took her things upstairs, but the bedroom door was locked. Some instinct took her higher in the house, to her old attic, and there her few possessions were dumped on the bed.

She took the mattress downstairs and aired it, and slept that night alone in her attic. And the two brothers became closer friends than ever, whispering and laughing to each other the whole evening long.

As summer drew nearer they began to do all kinds of housework. They would not let Effie make their meals or wash up after them. For the first time in her life she sat idle, and every time Bert saw her he would say loudly to Ronald: 'You see, she's not much good. We could do without her, quite well.'

She began to mope. 'What's the matter, Ronald? I 'aven't done anything wrong, 'ave I?'

Ronald did not reply.

At the end of May, Bert and Ronald became definitely uneasy. 'They'll be here any day now,' said Bert. 'She'd better go. What do you think?'

'You tell 'er.'

'Sound your aitches, now *they're* coming. You tell her. She's your missus, isn't she?'

'What 'ad I better do?'

'Sound your aitches, you fool.'

'We could send her away for a holiday,' said Ronald.

'That's an idea,' said Bert. 'Send her a long way. To London, say.'

The next morning, Bert said, with unfamiliar jocularity: 'We're sending you to London for a holiday, Effie.'

'Me?' she said, looking up from the range with wet eyes. 'I don't want an 'oliday. I only want to be let go on with my work, same as I always did.' She added, 'sir'.

'You'd better pack your things,' he said briefly. 'All of them. I'll lend you a case.'

' 'Ave I to?' she asked, looking at Ronald.

'Yes, you'd better,' he said, not looking at her.

So she put all her things into the case that Bert lent her, and the two brothers took her to the station and bought her a ticket. 'Here's two pounds for you,' said Ronald. 'Have a nice time. And don't come back,' he added, very gravely.

'Haven't I to come back?' she said.

'No,' said Bert, 'I shouldn't if I were you.'

'What shall I do, then?' she asked, taking her purse out of her bag and putting the folded notes in it.

'I don't know,' said Ronald.

'Come on,' said Bert, taking his arm. 'We haven't all day to stand here, you know.' He was thinking about Mrs Lonsdale, and Fay and Rita — the fat one and the thin one — wondering if they would have white dresses on and go for picnics in the Old Country, just as they had done in Vancouver. 'Come on, come on,' he said testily.

And the brothers walked up the platform without even shutting the carriage door.

X

I SLEPT in the same room as my sister until she died. Not only in the same room, but in the same bed. It was an ordinary, old-fashioned bed, brass and iron, one that we had had for a long time. I never remember the house without it. The rails at the top and bottom were round and black, broken in the centre by a brass thing, shaped like a heart, but with the point upwards. It was a very strong bed.

My sister and I were quite unlike. She was big and fair and athletic. She played tennis, and rowed. Once we went for a holiday to a place where there was a lake, and she rowed me round and round this until I was quite sick. I did not like the throaty sound of the water nor the dank smell of it, and it seemed to me that my heart began to move all about my body. Sometimes it even got into my calf. I thought, How shall I get home with my heart in my leg?

I am little and dark, and very, very thin. You would not notice me but that I have some good teeth. They are large, like white acorns, and I cannot quite close my mouth because of them. Yet they turn inwards rather than out.

I am sure my sister did not like me. I have seen her standing in front of the mirror, brushing her hair, which she wore long, and looking at me in the strangest way through the mirror as I lay in bed. She wore a white flannelette nightgown with a frilled collar and long sleeves. Sometimes the sleeves slipped upwards during the night and left a red mark on her arm. We did not talk much, but occasionally she would say quite roughly, 'What are you staring at?'

Of course, we went through a lot together — small things. Our parents died when we were in our twenties, and we were left to manage our own affairs. Or rather, we had a good solicitor, and he managed them. We went on sleeping in the same room, the same bed.

Our house was square and made of stone, and we kept hens. We used to quarrel sometimes about feeding them on winter mornings. And yet, hens must have their warm food. It smells nasty, but what of that? The smell of hen-food used to make my heart move about my body. Once, I know, it nearly got out of the tip of my left ear. How can that happen when the heart is so large and the ear so small? It is a complete mystery to me. Have you ever felt underneath a hen's foot? It is always so cold.

My sister was popular in a peculiar way. If there was anything to organize, anything to complain about, anyone's feelings to be trampled on, she would volunteer for the job. She would pull things together that had almost fallen to pieces. Her voice was slow, nasal and penetrating. She had high cheekbones, too. Now, I have no cheekbones at all. I have looked in the mirror, and felt for them, and not found them, and thought 'When I am a skeleton, I shall be quite unlike all the other skeletons'. But I have only patted my cheeks lightly, very lightly. Perhaps they are underneath.

I wanted to do so many things. I wanted to learn algebra, and, like many other people, I wanted to fly without wings, just by moving my elbows backwards and forwards, and dropping from a cliff or a high window. I am saving that for the future, however.

But one thing I did: I bought a harp at a sale. It was heavy, and the gilt on it was tarnished. I had it repaired and brought to the house, and when it was my sister's turn to feed the hens I would sometimes run my hands over the strings, from the bass where they said *gubble bub bub gubble* up to the highest notes which just went *pee ting*. I loved my harp so much that I was forced to sing. I do not have what is called a 'voice'. For some reason it does not sing the notes which are being played, yet it sounds very nice to me. When there was nobody in the house I would sing a great deal to my harp. I know I sang very loudly, but I did not think it mattered. One day my sister came in with some more people. I did not hear her until she came up to me and pulled my hair roughly, and said, 'Shut up! Do you want everybody to think you are mad?'

This was strange to me, as I had begun to think my sister was mad. Why did she row round and round lakes? Why did she play tennis, hitting at a ball that had to come back again, just a round, grey ball? Also, she had begun to have small black spots on her face, and when I looked at her I was forced to count them — one, two, three, four, five, six, seven, and so on.

We had but one servant, a very old woman called Hannah Luty. She had followed my mother, and altogether had worked with the family for nearly seventy years. She was very strong, but would not talk much. I do not remember hearing her put a sentence together except once. She spoke almost always in single words, and those with an effort. We all got on quite well together, though Hannah Luty would have nothing to do with the hens.

I would not be dominated by my sister, though she was older and bigger than me. In some ways she was like a horse, and as she grew older I began to think she was like a horse in bed, that I was sleeping with a horse. Sometimes I would lift the sheet from her face — she always slept with the sheet over her face — expecting to find a horse's head under it, a reddish horse's head with light hair. But I never did.

And yet I was happy. I loved the house, the hens, even Hannah Luty. I kept steadily on with my algebra, teaching myself from torn textbooks. It was very fascinating, for I never learnt what x was. If only I could find x, I thought, the whole world would become different. In the springtime, I used to look for x in birds' nests, when I was out walking, but in my secret heart I was a little ashamed. My wiser self told me it could not possibly be there. Yet I went obstinately on picking out the eggs one by one and replacing them.

My sister began following me around in a way I did not like. It was summer, and as I remember it, a very hot, dry summer. There was sometimes thunder without rain, and we both had headaches. I played my harp as often as I could, but I would no sooner get sat down on the stool beside it than my sister would come for me with one excuse or another. I tried getting up in the night, leaving her in what I thought was a deep sleep, but she would come down after me and get me back upstairs before I had time to draw my hands over the strings.

But everything came to an end the night my sister died. It was a summer night, late summer. The hay had been cut and was still lying. There had been so little rain that the thin grass was almost hay itself before it was cut. We had the windows of our room open, and the smell of hay came in, and was strong but pleasant.

Not long before, an electric cable had been brought over the land, and we had had the house wired, and had just begun to use the lights. We had two in our bedroom — a small lamp and a ceiling-light over the big mahogany dressing-table. There was a switch hanging down for the big light, but the lamp was on a table at my sister's side of the bed. I liked the light, and would often switch it off and on for pure pleasure. My sister slept soundly unless I moved from the bed. As soon as my feet touched the floor she would say uneasily, 'What are you doing? Where are you going?' She would sleep though the light went off and on a hundred times, and though I turned back the sheet to see if she had turned into a horse as many more. Yet she could tell if I left her side for one moment.

I was lying by my sister's side, thinking about *x* and smelling the smell of the hay. We had curtains that you could see through, and the black leaves on the trees outside shone through the thin curtains with a faint light. We are far from a town, though not so far from the main road, and everything was very silent this night.

Suddenly I heard something moving. Some creature was flying about in our room. Instead of being frightened, I was extra-ordinarily happy. I switched on the light and carelessly pulled the sheet from my sister's head. She was quite red in the face, but her neck was white. I looked up and saw a sort of pig flying about. It was a thin black pig, and it kept smiling at me, and it had teeth just like mine. All at once it swooped down to my sister's neck and began to bite and make horrible growling noises. My sister woke and jumped about like a fish I had seen on a river-bank, but she was not able to scream. It did not last very long. And then I grew cold and more frightened than death.

I jumped out of bed and pulled a drawer from the chest of drawers that stood in the corner opposite the door. And I emptied the clothes that were in it on to the floor and ran about trying to catch the flying pig in it. It wouldn't stay low and it wouldn't come near the floor. No, it kept tapping its bony wings on the ceiling, so I had to go after it.

There was only one way. I managed to stand on the bottom rail of the bed — oh! I can feel that iron tube under my instep still. In some way, I balanced the heavy drawer on the flat of my two hands, waiting until the grinning pig flew near, then I caught him up against the ceiling. How I laughed as I stood there! There was blood drying on my chin, and heavy blood soaking into my cotton night-dress. My sister looked so funny, quite unlike her usual self. I don't forget that sight, but she did not seem in the least like a horse any more.

I began to scream for Hannah Luty, and presently she came. My arms were tired with holding the drawer against the ceiling, and my feet hurt on the bedrail. Hannah always tied her head in a handkerchief for the night, and when she came into the room she screeched: 'Oh, God have mercy on our souls' — the only sentence I ever heard her say. I did not like her with her head tied up in a handkerchief.

The saddest part of all for me was when the policeman came and I told him I had caught the flying pig in the drawer. For he got me down so carefully, and shut the door and the windows, and lo, there was nothing in the drawer. Even I saw that there was nothing in the drawer! I began to cry, thinking what a lot of time I had spent standing on the bedrail, and how my arms ached and trembled.

I have never seen my harp since. I have an idea that my sister cut the strings with a linoleum knife some time before she died. I know now that I could have had it repaired, but I did not think of that at the time. I have not yet found x. The world seems to have closed in, and there are not many places left in which I can look for it.

Hannah

THE girl Hannah was seventeen, and she had made almost all that array of cakes and pastries on the kitchen dresser. She stood looking at them, her healthy pink face glowing with pride. She wore a blue dress and a white apron, and her hair waved down her back to her waist in a golden-brown shower.

The party should be a lovely one. All the girls from her Sunday-school class were coming, and four of the best-behaved boys as well. Then there was to be the young man, Thomas Henry Smithson, the one that all the girls secretly laughed at. Really, he was too conscientious, too lumberingly polite for anything. His hats seemed always small, his trousers tight, his boots big. But her mother liked him. He helped to make things go, sang a few songs in a voice he called baritone, and never lost his temper.

Hannah felt that she could put up with anything so long as Ralph Wellings turned up. He was nineteen. A strange boy for the little, fat, jolly parson to have as his son! Hannah had heard that he was wild, but he had never seemed wild to her. Sometimes they had met in the twilight, and he had walked along by her side through Pennyfoot woods to Hoyle's farm and carried the dozen eggs that she had gone to fetch back with him in a sugar-bag.

Of course, you were supposed to be still a child at seventeen, but Hannah didn't feel exactly like a child. She could talk to Ralph Wellings about the things she knew — the proper way to make candied toffee, the books she had recently found in the attic, old books in which all the letter esses were effs, the nicest hymn tunes. He never laughed at her, and she found this refreshing.

She loved him very much, admiring his forehead, for some reason, most of all. It was high and white. His blue-black hair, parted at the side, waved as beautifully as did hers. 'If we get married and have some children, they're sure to have curly hair,' she thought. She liked, too, his flecked hazel eyes and his long fingers with their triangular nails. He called her 'nice child', and always seemed glad to see her.

She took her entranced gaze from the cakes and went into the dairy. The house had once been a farm, and the cool, stone-shelved room was still called the dairy. One side of it was laden with food. There was a whole, crumb-browned ham on a dish by the side of meat-plate on which stood a perfectly cooked sirloin of beef. Another dish held four or five pounds of plump, cooked sausages. The trifles were ready, so were the stewed fruits for those who liked plainer sweets, and there was more cream, Hannah felt, than could possibly be used.

She ran out of the room, smiling with delight, to look for her mother.

'Are you getting ready, mother?' she called.

'Yes.'

Her mother stood, bare-armed, in front of the oval mirror, a worried look in her eyes, her mouth filled with steel hairpins. She had her skirt on, but her black satin bodice was flung over the curved bedrail.

'Aren't you washed, child?' She seemed to speak harshly because of the hairpins. 'The company'll be here before we know where we are. We sh'll have a rush, you'll see.'

'Never mind, mother, everything looks lovely. I wish the party was beginning just now.'

She ran out of the room and changed her dress in a perfect fury of speed. Her face was clean enough, her hands white. What was the use of washing over and over and over again? Now she was in the summer pink dress that made her look older than ever before. The skirt was flounced, and she jumped round ballooning it, running a comb through her hair at the same time.

'He'll like me, he'll like me, he will,' she chanted. And she ran across to her mother's room and flung herself panting on the great bed.

'Hannah, Hannah, be a lady!' cried her mother, rebukingly.

Hannah seemed to have been asleep for a long time. She woke slowly, feeling the grey light on her eyelids. Her hands, gnarled and shrunken, lay outside the blue-and-white coverlet. A shadowed white plait straggled over one shoulder, thinning to a thread-tied end as it reached her breast.

She moved a little, opened her eyes, and moistened her lips. The morning was sunny and still. It felt warm, warm. She dozed a little and went on thinking of the party her mother had given when she was seventeen. On that day Ralph Wellings had kissed her for the first time. Unknowingly she smiled. The pink dress with its flounces, she remembered that, too. How lovely it had all been.

She looked up when the door opened and frowned a little, seeing an ugly, middle-aged woman with a paper-backed book in her hand.

'Well, grandma,' the woman said in a kind and cheerful voice, 'I've been up a few times, but you were asleep. George is just going to the Post Office in the doctor's car, so will you sign the pension form? He's in a bit of a hurry. I'll help you up.'

She put a soft wrap about the old woman's shoulders and supported her while she wrote. 'H-a-n-n-a-h' she mouthed, then her attention was attracted by something else for a moment. She stared at the completed form and gave a fretful cry. 'Oh, grandma, you've gone and done it again! We sh'll have no end of bother. You've signed Hannah Wellings, and your name's Smithson — Smithson — Smithson.'

Home to Wagonhouses

A WOMAN, wearing a flat sage-green hat on the top of her white hair and a long, full raincoat over her spare figure, was riding slowly along on a bicycle. She had left her home at Wagonhouses over two hours ago, and was now tired and somewhat pale. Her usually sparkling brown eyes were dulled and anxious, as she was afraid she had missed her way. The yellow roads, narrow, grass-bordered, and hedged, had looked alike to her for the last five miles.

The time was summer, the day close and sunless, but there was a brilliant glare coming from the yellowish-grey sky. Each field seemed to be alive and panting for breath. Not a sound was to be heard except the stealthy squeak of the bicycle. All around stretched secret country, trees, fields, hedges, ditches, small mounds; bush-crowned, gentle depressions clothed with bramble in full leaf. But there was still no sign of a village.

Suddenly the character of the country changed. The road became rougher and hillier. At one time it ran between high rocks. A stream appeared from nowhere, and in its shrunken bed water flowed silently within a few feet of the road. Then it disappeared, a long hill ran downwards, and at the foot of this a few grey-roofed cottages stood. From one of them, standing near a bridge, a tall plume of smoke ascended and hovered almost unmovingly for a long time.

The woman gave a deep sigh, jumped off her bicycle, and stood looking into the valley. Then she wheeled the machine to the side of the road, laid it on its side, and sat down to eat from a parcel of sandwiches which she pulled from her pocket. She ate without any visible signs of pleasure.

The name of the woman was Sarah Ebbage, and she was on her way to see her husband, who had left her three years ago. He had come into some money then, and it had quite turned his head. She had heard that he was lying ill at Ebesham, and she wanted very much to see him.

When the money had first come, he had thought only of his wife, his children, his tiny farm. Then everything had grown too small for his ideas.

'We must move,' he said; 'we'll have a bigger place.'

He was a great broad-faced man, with blue eyes and yellow hair. He went about smiling, boasting, multiplying the few hundred pounds in his mind until it became almost a million. He went and looked at farms of fifty, a hundred, even three hundred acres, miles away from the place where he had been born and brought up. And on one of his journeys he met a widow called Mrs Alderson.

At first, he had talked of Mrs Alderson a great deal.

'It 'ud do you good to know a woman like that, Sarah. By, but she's a lively one, she keeps you laughing. And she's as smart as a carrot, too! The heels on her shoes are as high as that.' He measured off the length on his great hand.

Then he would look across at Sarah, his wife, noticing her soft, untidy hair, her preoccupied face, her work-worn hands, and unconsciously he would contrast with her Leemie Alderson. Leemie's real name was Amelia. She was in her thirties. She had black, curly hair. Even her fringe was curled, and she was always licking her first finger and going over her fringe curls delicately with the moistened tip of it.

Yes, he had talked a lot of Mrs Alderson, and wondered if it would be possible to have her stay with them for a week some time.

'There isn't room,' Sarah said to him in astonishment, 'and we've never had anyone to sleep here in twenty-five years.'

It was true. They had not. He wondered why he had ever thought of such a thing. They had two children. A boy, David, who was small and weakly, and who helped on the farm, and a girl, Mercia, as big and strapping as her brother was small, who taught in an infants' school in the nearest market town.

Mercia came home each week-end, so her room was always in readiness for her. Her clothes, washed by her mother, lay ready folded in drawer and wardrobe. She brought a small suitcase with her each Friday night. On Monday mornings she set off very early, sometimes before seven, but she was always full of life and spirits. It was quiet during the week without Mercia.

So David Ebbage stopped talking about Leemie Alderson, and began to think about her instead. They met a great deal. And one day they left quietly together, and in a roundabout way Sarah heard that they had set up house at Ebesham, several miles away. Mercia was angry, young David, said nothing at all, and Sarah went on with her work, as there was nothing else she could do.

Sarah Ebbage finished her sandwiches, staring down the hill at the cottage whose plume of smoke was now gone. She was certain that this was the house she had come to seek. David was lying there ill, and she was going to see him at last, after three years. She had thought this out over many sleepless nights. She would go up to the door and knock. Would it be open or shut? That didn't matter. The black-haired woman would come, her face blank and staring, seeing a stranger.

'Can I speak to — er — David?' she would say. And, perhaps, 'I'm a relation'.

She would smile and say 'Please'. Surely the woman would let her in.

She got up from the roadside, her knees trembling a little. To steady them, she walked down the hill, wheeling her bicycle. There was no noise coming from the houses, not a sign of life. The blood rushed to her face, flushing it, and her heart thumped in her side with increasing violence. She had a gentle soul, and very much feared the coming interview with the woman who had taken her husband from her.

But it had to be. Leaning her bicycle against the hedge, she walked up the path to the open house door. The garden had not been weeded for some time. It was lush and overgrown. Yellow tea-roses hung heavily from a tree that had once been carefully nailed to the wall. The strips of felt had rotted away from their nails and never been replaced. The place smelt of decay.

'He must have been ill for a long while,' she thought, knocking timidly.

She waited, her hands clenched. Nobody answered. She knocked louder. Still nobody came. But she thought she heard a slight sound from upstairs.

'Hello', she called, and again she thought she heard a movement of some kind; but no voice answered her.

She stepped inside, still calling 'Hello', and found herself in a large kitchen. There was a square table with a greyish cloth over half of it, on which flies were quietly creeping. Soiled dishes stood everywhere, even the sink slab that she could see through the open scullery door was filled with them. A green glass vase on the windowsill contained several dead roses, and a wasp buzzed angrily above them and bumped itself in a reasonless way against the glass of the window. That was now the only noise.

Sarah Ebbage felt sick as she looked about, and saw her husband's cap lying on a red couch. It was the same cap he had worn three years ago about the farm. She took it between her hands and unconsciously pressed it.

Acting on some determined impulse, she put down the cap, went back to the door, and mounted the bedroom stairs. There was no banister rail on the sharp rise of the wall, but a wide greasy line showed at hands' height. She climbed upwards proudly without touching the wall.

At the top, on her left, a brown curtain hung over a doorway. She lifted this, and stood blinking into a frowsy bedroom. There was a dusty red carpet on the floor — this she saw first of anything — and a tumbled bed on which somebody was lying. The curtains at the window were still undrawn. A mirror gleamed dimly in a corner, and beneath it, on the dressing-table, stood a jumble of scent bottles, dirty brushes and combs, and a few soiled handkerchiefs.

She sniffed the fusty air uncertainly, and said in a low voice, 'Are you there, David?'

'Yes,' replied the man on the bed.

She moved forward with more certainty now. First she pulled back the curtains, letting in the blinding glare of the day, then she tried to push up the sash of the window.

'It won't open,' said the voice behind her.

She turned round, blinking back the film from her eyes, and saw her husband lying under a patchwork quilt. His head was on a dirty pillow, and his fine yellow hair was almost the colour of ashes. His eyes had sunk into two hollows under high cheekbones, and his lips clung together beneath a straggling moustache. He had not been shaved for some days, and his beard sparkled with a golden light.

'David,' she said, 'whatever did ye do it for?'

'Nay, lass, I don't know,' he answered in a weak voice.

'Where's *she*?' Sarah jerked her head towards the window.

'Across at Mrs Tyson's, mebbe. Sometimes I don't see her the day long. I've had my breakfast, though. She brought that.' He pointed to a sticky lacquer tray on the floor.

Sarah stood by the bedside, looking down at her husband. She put out her hand and stroked his arm. Her eyes were mild and firm and had lost all their tired look. She saw that he was wearing an old blue shirt and had a ring on his finger that was now much too large for him. Yes, he must have been ill a long time. A pity she hadn't heard sooner.

'D'you want to come home, David?'

He took her hand in both his and pressed it to his rough cheek. For some time he remained silent.

'Will you have me back, Sarah?'

'Of course.'

She would find some way of getting him home immediately. Tyre marks were on the road: perhaps somebody had a car or a lorry. It would be a nuisance about the bicycle, but that could always be fetched.

'How can we get you?'

They talked softly for a while; then she went downstairs to heat some milk for him. She took off neither her flattish green hat nor her raincoat, and she ignored the soiled dishes. She was now calm and serene, unafraid of meeting the black-haired widow.

When her husband had drunk the milk, she went downstairs again and rode in an unhurried way to a farm about a quarter of a mile farther along the road. When she came out of the yard some time later, she was driving a long, flat hay wagon to which was hitched a lumbering brown horse. 'So David has made some friends,' she was thinking reflectively, grateful to the big farmer who had unhesitatingly granted her request.

'Mind you, I'm wanting it, but I'm glad to 'blige David.'

'My son will come back straight away with the wagon. I'll leave my bicycle, and he can ride home on that,' she said. But she was not thinking what she was saying. Her whole brain was busy with plans of how to get David dressed and away out of the house.

She drew up at the cottage gate. Still there was no sign of life.

'Sarah?' called her husband as she entered the door.

'Yes, it's me, lad,' she answered him. 'I've got it.'

She was looking round. She would take the bedding, a couple of cushions from the couch, even the thick tablecloth, anything to make David comfortable for the journey. She would send everything back. Young David could call: 'My mother's sent these back, please, and thank you.'

The stream of her love, which had been dammed for three years, gushed forth again. He was ill, her husband, the poor lamb. Ill and uncared for. Of course she would take him back. Wasn't that what she had really come for this morning? Not with fine-brushed hair and high-heeled shoes, but in her old working clothes she had hurried to fetch him. And he longed to be home.

She helped him into his suit, guiding his big feet and shrunken legs through the hollow tunnels of his blue trousers. He made faint, sad sounds of dissent as she tucked in his shirt and fastened his braces, 'Nay, lass, I s'll never be able to manage.'

'Of course you will.'

Sarah was trembling with the effort of moving him. He was iller than she thought. 'I've got the cart all comfortable. You'll be on the road in five minutes if you just make up your mind. Come, come, lad.' She chided him gently.

When at last she got him on to the flat cart, they were both wet with sweat. Sarah was breathing quickly as she gathered the reins in her hands. What if that woman should come now, should make a scene, demanding her tablecloth, her dirty pillows? Then she tossed her head, clicked to the horse, and set off up the hill for home.

David Ebbage lay sunk in his improvised bed. The effort of moving had wearied him, and the cart creaked and jolted. He began to think over his life. He thought of Mercia, and young David, wondering how they had taken his departure, how they would like his return. He thought of Leemie, first as a red, angry face near him screaming: 'Yes, you would, you would get ill. All your own money's spent, now you think you can live on what I've got,' then as the laughing, provocative creature he had first met, then she faded out like a dream, and he was near Sarah, his wife, with whom he had lived for twenty-five years.

He opened his eyes and looked at her. What a good, strong pink face she had. How straightforward was the look in her brown eyes. Her hair was even whiter — it had turned early, he remembered —

but now his own matched it.

Sarah sat up straight, gazing in front of her at the horse's wide flanks. The air was closer still, the sky like blinding white glass. She suddenly remembered how silent the day had been, and longed for the pleasant noises of the farmyard, the creaking bray of the pump, the clatter of young David's clogs as he crossed the flagged yard. Wagonhouses again. Home. Home, with David there. No use wondering how long he'd be there. Life wasn't just a matter of years.

Proud and smiling, she looked down at the emaciated figure by her side. Her husband was whispering something. 'Sarah, Sarah, you won't leave me. You'll never leave me, will you?'

'No,' she answered, serene and sure, 'I'll never leave thee.'

Eve

THE GIRL called Eve stepped off a bus and stood for a minute looking up a quiet suburban street. The sky above was dim with the dull blue of a summer evening, and very few stars were out. There were youngish trees planted at intervals of a few yards along the pavement, and now and then a cool wind rustled their leaves. When the noise of the bus had died away, there was not another sound. The street went uphill, and vanished in a kind of horizon darkness.

The girl was dressed in black, but not the black of mourning. She was tall and slight, with hair so light that it looked unnatural; yet it was straight, and shone silkily. Her face was pale, her eyes long rather than large, and her lips made her look beautiful. She held herself erect, there was pride in her shoulders and ankles. Most people would look twice at her. She rarely looked twice at anybody.

When she was tired of standing she began to walk slowly up the left-hand side of the street. There were wooden palings, and gardens of a few yards' length. Here and there bunches of darkish flowers showed up amid the darker green. The strong scent of stocks came up her nostrils.

'Just the same,' she murmured to herself.

She carried a small black bag under her arm. It was empty except for a handkerchief and a mirror, a pencil and a notebook. It had been heavier, she recollected, when she got on the bus; but there had been five pennies in it then.

She bent down to open the low gate of her home garden, gently breathing 'Company?' as she noticed the lighted windows. 'Well, well. And will dear mother be pleased to see me?'

She rang the bell of the front door, and through glass panels saw the stout reluctant figure of her stepmother come into the rosy light of the hall-passage. She saw, too, the fat, ball-topped banister rail that guarded the stairs like a sentinel, and remembered the many times she had slipped her cool palm over its polished smoothness.

'Oh, it's you!' The quiet and bitter voice of the second Mrs Gallon seemed to shrivel a small, inoffensive rose which was growing near a kind of drainpipe. 'We have visitors tonight, important visitors.'

Eve laughed. 'That's all right. I don't mind. I can stand anything.'

The older woman's head settled firmly back into her neck. She sniffed. 'Have you been drinking?'

Eve laughed again. 'You know it's customary to have wine with one's dinner.'

'Faugh!'

There was a movement inside, by the drawing-room door, which was less than four yards away, and Dorfy, one of the twins, looked out. She blushed when she saw the visitor, and said, 'Hullo, Eve'.

'Hullo. Is father in?'

She was glad when her father came shuffling up to the door, blinking behind his glasses; the same as ever, his soft white beard faintly stained with nicotine, his newest suit looking old and creased already. She noticed that he was smoking a cigarette instead of his pipe, and that he smoked it as if he were sucking it, breathing up his nose at the same time. But that might have been just nervousness.

'Is that Eve?'

He stood behind his massive wife, and puffed away at the unaccustomed cigarette so quickly that half an inch of ash formed and fell before he said 'Come in'.

'What a nice welcome,' Eve said, gently pushing past Mrs Gallon. 'Why, *mother* dear! You always made me say mother, didn't you? What's the matter?'

For one minute, Mrs Gallon had held her arm stiffly almost across the width of the passage, as if she were defending something.

'Who is with us tonight? Dear Dr Pilchard, or dear Captain Gramp?'

A red flush rose almost to Mrs Gallon's eyes, and she said in a choking whisper: 'No. But they are two very nice young men. One is an architect, and the other is in a bank. And if you must come in, I hope you will behave yourself. Do you know that Captain Gramp has never been near since that night you came last?'

'No?'

'You know the reason why very well.'

Suddenly she changed her manner as a rather noisy cough came from the nearby drawing-room. 'Yes, do come in. Shall I take you upstairs first?'

'No, thanks. I'm not staying long. Has Marjorie got a very bad cold?'

Her father had almost backed into the drawing-room, and soon Eve was inside, being introduced to the two young men. One was burly, rather like a boxer, only his feet were big and clumsy. The other was small and thin, with a long neck and sloping shoulders and a rather astonishing head of black, curly hair. Their names were Roy Cough and Smithfield Hullah.

As soon as she heard what they were called, Eve leaned back in her chair in silent enjoyment and closed her eyes.

'Marjorie,' she said, softly. The other twin was Marjorie, and she was always called Pet. Eve had managed to call Dorothy Dorfy all her life, as the others did, but she could not say Pet, any more than she could call the boy Gerald Boysie, as his mother did.

Marjorie came and stood near her stepsister's chair.

'Which is yours, the boxer or the bottle?'

Marjorie stood there, big and uneasy, a younger edition of her mother. Her hair was waved, she was even corseted. She would never grow old, because she was old already.

'We were just going to have some music,' she said stiffly. 'Mr Hullah sings.'

'So it's the bottle,' said Eve, without opening her eyes. 'Has he brought his music. And talking of music, did you read Beachcomber's bit about Wagner's second wife?'

Nobody spoke.

'Well, she was so musical that once when she came to a five-barred gate she stopped in front of it and sang all the spots on her veil.'

She opened her eyes and for a long time looked up and down a yellow satin stripe on the wallpaper. Marjorie walked away and sat down beside her twin.

Mr Hullah was standing near the black piano, unrolling his music with rather sweaty hands. He and Mr Cough were Smithy and Royboy to each other, and had sung many duets together. They started off immediately with 'Watchman, what of the night?'

While they sang, the girl Eve, dismissing them without effort, walked along a country lane in an almost gold-coloured linen dress, swinging a green-dotted milk-jug on her finger. At one point of the road there was a strange and disturbing smell that poured out from a hidden plant. She always thought it was a nettle, but it might not have been. Yet at this moment, she used to turn and take the warm hand of the man who walked by her side. The thatched roof of the barn on their left, the thatched roof of the farm on their right, seemed to have been etched on the inner side of her eyelids.

'All this will last for ever and ever and ever.'

Behind the door of the furnished cottage was a child's coat-hanger, on which was printed in pale letters 'Boy Blue'. He would put down the milk-jug and the egg packet, and swing her round by the shoulders and kiss her, and once she thought 'Hold thou Boy Blue before my closing eyes' and asked if it was blasphemy.

Or they were coming through the Pyrenees in the train, waiting for dinner. Hungry, about to be satisfied, wanting to get out and walk, yet knowing too much to snatch at heaven. The round, red September moon seemed to be looking at them in a surprised way. She was enraptured.

'Why, the moon always has the same kind of face, wherever we are.'

Yet she was not really thinking of the moon.

And the slight, fair English boy in the corner kept on crumbling his bread and telling them in a quivering voice that he had been living in Burgos for a whole year, and that he was going home for a holiday. He seemed to weep with joy at hearing his own language.

She had been much younger then.

'Watchman, what of the night?' died away in a surge of emotion, and Dorfy and Pet clapped quite loudly, leaning forward until their chairs creaked, and smiling at each other. They were already visualizing a life of calmness, and chintz, and small dogs, music, and cards. Mrs Gallon had tiptoed out to see how the woman who 'came in' was managing with the coffee and sandwiches. Sometimes the coffee was palatable, sometimes it was undrinkable. One never knew.

The singers, hardly acknowledging the applause, went hurriedly on into 'Come to the fair'. This was to be followed by 'Maire, my girl', and 'It was only a tiny garden'. Eve made them feel flustered and uneasy, so they hid themselves behind their songs. The man with the clumsy feet played the piano with hands almost as clumsy. And after a while, he and his friend grew warm and lordly, and stared into the glazed eyes of the twins, bawling 'Little white bride, on your snow-white pillow', without meaning anything at all.

They were out rowing on the loch, smoking to keep away the midges. There was an island, with a small castle on it. They never asked anything about it, never wanted to go on the island, just as they would never stop to look into the middle of a crowd, sensing a fight or an accident. The world went on around them.

'I don't want to go fishing. I don't want to step on a beetle. I don't even want to kill a midge.'

'Neither do I.'

'No. Only fleas, Et cetera.'

He laughed. She could still hear his laugh, and the rhythmic plash of the oars, and feel the coldness of the water creep up her bare arms almost as far as her shoulders. She had simply forgotten to bring a wrap.

And afterwards the warmish, sweaty smell of his tweed coat would surround her.

Dorfy poked her triumphantly, pleased with her silence.

'Don't they sing beautifully? Come on, we're going to have coffee and sandwiches in the dining-room.'

Eve rose from her chair gracefully, and stood up, tall as a young tree: looking at her stepsisters, her stepmother smiling archly in the doorway, her father, old, squeezed, trodden on, and at the two young men who might, or might not, marry Dorfy and Pet. She had not taken off her hat, nobody had asked her to, and she had forgotten it, yet it stamped her stranger. She still carried the almost empty black bag under her arm.

Even on the way to the dining-room she remembered a hurried

lunch in Rotterdam, and a waiter who kept pushing wizened fruit under their noses, crying 'Do have a little orensh', proud of his command of languages. Trams, and ships' masts, and train windows gravely closed, remembered. And then some kind of a quick change, as if both their brains were being stirred with a spoon. A realization, a quick parting, no time then to think of the golden frock, the green-spotted milk-jug. Only a long silence.

She ate a lot of sandwiches, grimly, and waited just as grimly until the visitors had left, and Boysie Gerald had been brought home in some girl's car.

'I can go up and see my old room, I suppose?' she asked, smiling the sort of smile that used to make the second Mrs Gallon smack her face when she was younger. The second Mrs Gallon had to restrain herself, or she would have smacked the girl's face now.

'You can go up and look at it. I didn't know you were sentimental. And in any case, I've turned it into a boxroom. We don't keep a spare room. I sold the bed months ago.'

'I see.'

Eve kept on smiling in her stepmother's face, but though her lips were parted until her teeth showed, there was no sign of a smile in her eyes. The blue shadows of tiredness on her face deepened. She began to hum 'Watchman, what of the night?' in a throaty imitation of Mr Hullah, then stopped, and turning, called 'Good night, girls. Good night, Gerald.'

'Good night,' they chorused.

'I'll just say good night to father.'

Her father was still in the dining-room. He had filled his pipe with fresh tobacco, and was smoking away, quickly and nervously, as if he knew that his wife would come in any minute and drag him off unwillingly to bed. Shreds of tobacco had fallen on the table, but he could not see them with his weak eyes.

His daughter Eve flicked them on to the floor with her neat, black-gloved hand. In a quiet whisper she asked, 'Have you some money, father? Quickly, quickly.'

'Why, no, I haven't any, Eve. I never go out, you know, and your — your mother gets my tobacco with the groceries.'

'Oh, poor father, is it as bad as that?'

She had recovered from her haste, her fright, whatever it was that had possessed her to whisper a need so quickly. And she smiled because the second Mrs Gallon stood in the doorway, looking at the father and daughter, at the old man's smoke-crowned head, at the girl's gloved fingers.

'It's late.'

'Yes, it is. Very late.'

And the girl Eve went out of the room, opened the outer door and walked down the path, calling a soft and smiling good night. Then she shivered involuntarily because the air had grown colder and her clothing was thin, and there was no thick tweed coat being placed over her braced shoulders. She closed the garden gate behind her and walked down the street at her ordinary pace. The night was filled with distant stars and other people's flowers.

Landlord of the Crystal Fountain

A TALL, good-looking, red-haired school teacher of about thirty stood in King's Cross Station one Friday afternoon trying to find enough change for her ticket. She had a violent headache, and frowned as she fumbled in her brown leather bag.

Her name was Brenda Millgate, and she was going north for the week-end to see her sister. It was purely a visit of duty; she had nothing whatever in common with Doris, and she looked upon the week-end as wasted already.

Nothing would go right for her. A few coppers rolled from her fingers, and she felt embarrassed as obsequious strangers handed pennies back to her. But at length the ticket was bought, and she picked up her week-end case and walked resolutely on to Platform Ten. The bookstall was further down on her left, but she felt too tired to go down and buy any of the alluring-looking magazines offered for sale. There was not much time. She had had to hurry as it was. And now she found the train was crowded.

She was dressed very neatly in brown, and had on a cream-coloured blouse with buttons that very nearly matched the colour of her hair. She had also a brown silk umbrella with a shining orange knob on it, and there was an orange leather band across her brown handbag.

In spite of her knowledge that she looked both well and intelligent, there seemed to be no room for her. There was a place or two in the non-smoking carriages, but she did not like the stink that came out of them. 'You can get the smell of smoke out of your clothes,' she thought, 'but not that — that other.' She did not know what to call it. But though she walked quickly up and down the platform in her brown shoes, she could find nowhere suitable, and had to jump up and stand in the corridor at last. Just behind her, she heard a loud, hearty voice saying something that was followed by a burst of laughter. She put down her case, and watched the bookstall glide smoothly past the window. Then she turned her head to see how many people were in the carriage behind her.

Why, there was a seat! In fact, only five men were sitting down, but five such big men she had never before seen together. They seemed to fill the place to overflowing. Probably there were lots more seats on the train, but her head was so bad that she could hardly see them. The door of the carriage opened, and a friendly voice said, 'Do come in here, miss. There's plenty of room.'

'Thank you,' she said gratefully. She felt tired enough to faint or to fall asleep.

The five big men rearranged themselves and let her sit in a corner seat near the window. For a few minutes they gave her all their attention until they had her settled and comfortable. One put her case on the rack, another even helped her off with her hat, the one opposite moved so that she could put her feet up on the seat, the fourth asked her if she would like a paper to read, and the fifth one stood up laughing and said, 'Now we're all comfortable, aren't we?'

She sank back with a sigh of relief. 'I've got such an awful headache. This is lovely, lovely.'

One of them made a joke about her red hair, and she laughed softly. 'You're all together, aren't you?' she asked. 'Friends?'

'Yes, friends,' they answered, and one of them said 'All together.'

She sank almost immediately into a kind of stupor, in which she could hear the dulled rattle of the train wheels and the quiet hum of voices. 'Why are these men so pleasant?' she wondered. 'So steeped in comfortableness?' It felt nice to be with them.

After a short while she woke, feeling much better, and began to study her fellow-travellers. 'What great hulking men,' she thought, 'and yet how considerate they are.' Not one of them had started to smoke.

'Smoke if you like,' she said. 'I like the smell. But first of all, do tell me what you are. What do you do? I've been wondering ever since I saw you.'

The man in the far corner leaned forward. He had thinning black hair brushed as far as it would go round a dome-like forehead.

'We're landlords, my girl,' he said. 'Landlords, all of us. We've every one got licensed houses.'

'Pubs,' her mind flashed.

'You're all very big landlords,' she said.

He wagged his finger at her, 'Ah, it's the life.' He took out a pipe and filled it, and began to smoke.

'Tell me the names of your — your houses,' she said.

'The Golden Lion at Firley Green; The White Horse at Itterington; The Case is Altered (that's a puzzler, isn't it, miss?) just at the entrance to Hay Park; The Crown, Bridge Road.'

They were all busy, but one, pulling card-cases out of their pockets. 'We've been up to a convention; a spree, by God. Hush, we've had the time of our lives!'

Then she looked across at the man who sat opposite, the one who had moved so that she might put her feet up. He was, she thought, the tallest of them all. He had a red face and tight, straw-coloured curls thick over his head. His eyes were blue-grey. He wore a dark suit and a black tie. He had not yet spoken. 'What's the name of yours?'

'I'm proud of the name of mine,' he said, 'but I haven't any cards on me.'

The others all handed their cards to her, and she took them impatiently, leaning forward, looking at the straw-haired giant, whose deep voice had at the same time pleased and startled her. 'What is it? What's the name of yours?'

'All in good time,' he said, smiling slowly. 'It's called the Crystal Fountain.'

Then the others began to talk about their homes and their lives. They discussed their wives, and announced themselves as henpecked men, all but the landlord of the Crystal Fountain, who kept silent. He and Brenda sat looking at each other in perfect contentment, listening to the talk around them.

Casually they brought out stacks of sandwiches, and made her share them. At first, she was full of dismay. Sandwiches — dry sandwiches in a train! Yet presently she was eating one of salmon and cucumber.

'But this is real salmon,' she cried in astonishment, 'and the cucumber's as fresh as a drink of water.'

'Of course it is,' one shouted. 'We know what to buy and where to buy it.'

'You didn't get them near here, I'll bet.'

'But we did. And within a stone's throw of King's Cross, too.'

The sandwiches melted away like snow in a thaw. There was enough for everybody. Brenda got plenty of compliments — on her height, on her appetite, on her red hair. She blushed with pleasure.

After the meal, they all relaxed, leaning back and unfastening buttons that had become too tight. One or two smoked. The dome-headed one offered her cigarettes, and when she refused one, he was glad.

'Not speaking in a business way, of course,' he said. 'I've nothing against it. We see it, practically speaking, every evening of our lives. It wouldn't do for us to be prejudiced. But I'm glad.'

Brenda slipped her feet down from the opposite seat, sighing with joy. She had not the least idea why she now felt so happy.

'I've never met any landlords socially,' she thought. 'No, I've never met a landlord before in my life. Publicans. Publicans and sinners. Perhaps they were like this when Jesus was alive. No wonder He . . .' She dozed again.

She thought of her life, of her mother's ambition that she should be a teacher. She thought with astonishment of the examinations she had passed, the years of pleasant training. She was not in the least clever. She had no retentive memory. But somehow everything had come to her. Flukes, flukes. And she *was* good with children — just plain good at getting on with people, with the heads, with her fellow teachers.

And because she had liked the children who flowed under, rather than passed through her hands, and had spent her time hoping that here and there a silk purse dwelt among the pigs' ears, she had not thought a great deal about men.

There was one who thought of her, and she knew it. But she was not in any way satisfied with him. He was shorter than she was — small, dark, dry and meticulous. He liked her to be a kind of imitation of himself. He had the power of making her feel that she would eventually marry him; that one day, when she was tired and sick of school and all that it meant, she would turn to him. So he simply waited.

She did not dislike him physically. She was tolerant, and adaptable, ready to make the best of anything. His name was Claud Foden.

She opened her eyes and looked across at the landlord of the Crystal Fountain. He was studying her gravely. He leaned forward and spoke quietly. 'My God,' he said, 'but you're a nice woman. I suppose you're more a lady, though.'

'No,' she answered him just as quietly, 'woman's the word,' and soon she was telling him about herself.

'My father kept a shop. Well, my stepfather, and Doris — that's my sister — and I went to school on his money. He was a butcher, a big fine man with curly hair like yours, only white. I don't remember my own father. My mother always used to tell us that she had married again so that we could have a good education. She didn't know much, but she was ambitious. I'm supposed to know a lot, but I'm not ambitious that way, at all. I'm a teacher, but I've just begun to wonder why I'm a teacher, for my heart isn't in it. It's with the children, all right, but not with what I'm supposed to be teaching them.'

She felt astonished to hear these words coming from her mouth. She did not usually talk like that. No, she used a sort of jargon, a 'we're all girls together' kind of language. Anything to crush down her height and healthiness, her over-exuberance. She really envied the dim creatures who tripped about like neat mice, knowing she could never grow like them. Her red hair was thick and curly, and it shone; when she saw it in a mirror, she knew that it was beautiful, but always thought disparagingly of people who liked that kind of thing.

The two sat looking at each other, admiring each other. The other four men were talking among themselves. They leaned back, stretching out their legs. Their firm calves touched each other, so that their blood seemed to flow through one body rather than two. They kept on looking at each other with absorbed pleasure as the train rushed through the gathering darkness.

Brenda began to think dreamily that she would like to have a dressing-gown of orange and green, and a link of great amber beads like lumps of sucked toffee. And imitation pearls — only they must be great big ones, too. She would like to have rings on her fingers, 'and bells on my toes' she murmured, and dangling gold ear-rings.

'And now listen to me,' the man opposite said, in his voice that could be deep and quiet at the same time, 'for I've got a lot to say to you. I don't know much about you — you're not married, by any chance, are you?'

'No.'

'Well, I have been, to a fine girl, none better. For five years. But she's dead now. She's gone and can't be brought back. I'm wanting another wife. I'm wanting her quick, and I think you'll do. What do you say?'

'You'll have to let me think.'

'Well, don't take long, then, for we haven't far to go. I want you to come with me to see the place, but you'll like it. I've no fear of that. I like it. It's out at Ella Syke, on the moor edge. You might find it a bit quiet, but I don't. What do you say, lass?'

She was thinking, 'This can't often happen to people. It's never happened to anyone I know. But I'm going to do it.'

A silence had fallen over the carriage. She said, 'All right, then, as soon as you like.'

'That's good.'

'I'll have to send a telegram to Doris. She's expecting me. But do you think I'd make you a good wife — in a business way, I mean?' She had no other qualms.

'I'll soon teach you. But you might have been born to it.' He stood up and presented her gravely to his four friends. 'Any one of them'll vouch for me,' he said. 'There's no underhand business here. And I expect to call and see your sister in a day or so. We'll make a special day of the wedding.'

The five big men took everything for granted, and fell to talking again, while the girl leaned back and thought. There would certainly be a lot of fuss about her job. Doris would be astounded. It would mean a fresh start in life. She would never see Claud Foden again as long as she lived.

On the other hand, this new bliss that had grown up in her would never leave her. She was ready to go on. 'It'll be hard work, and different work, but I'll do it.' There must be some of her mother's ambition in her, she thought. Here it was. Her eyes blazed with a new light.

She carried her own case, because he had one of his own. They walked across the grey northern station to find a telegraph office behind the closed Post Office. But he took hold of her arm with his free hand, and she liked the firm way it held her. Yet she could think of nothing to put in the telegram except: 'Don't worry about me. I am going to the Crystal Fountain.'

Honeymoon

THEY were used to the different bedrooms by now. The first —
that marvellous, soul-less, linen-sheeted home — had a bathroom
of the whitest and cleanest next door. 'You go, darling' (some day,
we'll have a bath with silver taps in, she thought). 'No, you, my
darling.' And he would sing in spite of all the other people; and she
would lie on the top of the new eiderdown, cooling her burning face
on the warm pillow, listening to the tones of his voice and
absorbing them.

On the third morning, they thought of money. The bill was
surprisingly big, and they were not quite sure about tips.
Downstairs, Bruce left two shillings under a plate, two separate
shillings, one for the meek waiter, and one for the arrogant. But
that one had come and stood beside them when they paid, like a
large and stubborn hippopotamus. So the meek waiter must have
taken both of the shillings. 'I'm glad,' Bruce said simply, putting
all the change in his pocket.

The second bedroom was in a tiny cottage. Heavenly luck. It
was owned by Mrs Moyce and her sister. There was a long garden,
filled with cabbages and honeysuckle. Mrs Knockton, at the
Floating Light, made their tea, but she didn't want them for the
night. And they had been sent to the Floating Light by a woman
miles away, who had flung up her hands to emphasize how
scrupulously clean Mrs Knockton was. Mrs Knockton just said, 'I
don't mind a *man* now and again, but we're so *busy*, you see, and it's
noisy in the evenings. Well, if you please, I'd *rather* not, you being a
couple. But there's Mrs Moyce.'

They whispered and grinned a lot — too much — at Mrs
Moyce's, because of a photograph over the bed of an old man with
a long white beard and a naughty little twinkle in his eye. And they
would linger in the mornings, bathing in cold water and a small
slippery china bowl, and Mrs Moyce would shout 'Come, come,'
in a warning voice, 'breakfast is cold.'

Breakfast was always cold at Mrs Moyce's; the bacon hard, the boiled eggs tepid. And there were astonishing things on the table, beetroot, and dripping lettuce, and tomatoes as small as nuts. Julie would pass hot tea to Bruce, and when he had put his cup down, pick up his hand and smell it gravely, and think a complete advertisement, because of the carbolic. And she thought of herself, too, at the age of fourteen, scrubbing the front door step with the same kind of soap.

In spite of the cold bacon, it was lovely at Mrs Moyce's. The woman grew to care for them alarmingly. She brought cups of tea for them at eight o'clock, and hurled her dark blue bosom up the narrow, polished steps each time Bruce slipped down them. 'Be careful, my child, my child. I've warned you, over and over again.' Her timid sister was Miss Lippincott. She had black hair which looked as if it was tied across the top of her head, and she said 'Oh!' in a quiet, unhappy way if the couple came upon her accidentally.

Each day they went out and walked until they could hardly put one foot before another, singing 'Sweet Adeline' in the empty spaces. And however late they got in, there was Mrs Moyce, sitting knitting and listening to a tinny, muffled wireless machine. But she would get up and give them salty ham for supper, and only cold water to drink. And they would wake up with parched mouths at dawn, and creep out for more drinks of water, and look out of the window at the new, dark green hills covered with curls of mist, and listen to the loud, careless voices of the birds.

And she would dreamily and yet with purpose pull her thin nightdress over her head. Somewhere, sometime, it would drop on the floor or on the pillow behind her. She would feel its light silkiness leaving her smooth fingers, and abandon herself without effort to the gulf that was no gulf, but a warm, rushing, upcarrying whirlwind; a wind that would presently leave her spent upon some newer shore; that turned astonishingly into Mrs Moyce's black and brass bed, with Mrs Moyce's deceased and yet so very much alive father musing down from his glass frame; even into the face of Mrs Moyce, and her green lacquer tray with the two cups of tea and the pink sugar-bowl; and the excited, warning voice of Mrs Moyce, with her 'Eight o'clock, young people', and its undercurrent of 'I know'.

'She's her father's daughter. Perhaps she does.'

Bruce would light a cigarette, and Julie would keep on smiling at him, not having to answer; liking him more and more, knowing that she knew less about him each day, but not worrying.

He was clever. So much she had decided in her own mind. But frighteningly aloof. He said very little. Everything he read stayed documented in his mind, ready to be brought out at any time, discussed seriously. She had read hundreds, thousands of books, and they had flowed away from her like seen streams. With an effort, she might recall snatches of them, ripples of rats swimming, trout (always so much smaller than people said), a black waterhen calling to its lone chick. But who should trouble about books, with all the world open before them?

And surprisingly, in the middle of the honeymoon, came an interlùde. There was one black flaw in Mrs Moyce's. She had had something sanitary installed in the garden, and you came out of it reeking all over with creosote. They would talk for a long time, enviously, about sweet earth-closets they had known, at the end of long gardens.

'And sitting there, with the door open, watching bees . . .'

'And butterflies, going quietly . . .'

'And bluebottles like business men . . .'

'Or very wet rain, and a blackbird jumping out of the apple blossom . . .'

'Or even ours behind the big gate at home, with a taper stuck in a crack of the wood, and spiders to watch.'

So they put their three-and-elevenpenny packs, that were always bursting in strange new places, on their backs again, and said goodbye to Mrs Moyce, full of warmth because her bill was so small. The meek sister had hidden, they feared, in the creosote place, out of shyness; and they rushed away, forgetting to blow a kiss to the old man over the bed, lest Miss Lippincott should suffocate.

They walked into Shaftesbury, and then out of it to find a railway line.

'Let's go on a train, for a change.'

It was thrilling, she thought, not knowing where you were to sleep.

In the afternoon, when the sun was hot and they had walked far enough, they stopped an imposing bus called Greyhound. The fare was a great deal, and she whispered as the conductor made out long, written tickets, 'Why does it cost so much?' and Bruce answered 'I don't know. Perhaps this is young Alf Greyhound, helping the business on.'

Listening to them, laughing behind them and sucking his pipe, was Blaize Dickinson. Soon the three of them were talking over the roar of the bus.

'Where are you two going?'

'We don't know. Just anywhere. We've booked to Dorchester.'

'Would you like to see my place?'

'Would we?'

They turned to each other, shining-eyed. They had only met Blaize once or twice in London, casually in Charles's bookshop, and had not even bothered to wonder where he lived. This would be lovely.

They climbed out of the bus, and stood like awkward children, waiting for Blaize to tell them which way to go.

'Across the road and down this lane.'

They looked at two clean cottages, waiting to say 'Oh' and 'How nice', but there was a long way to go. He took them across a common that was like no common she had ever seen before; smooth-turfed, dotted with bramble bushes and sheltering trees. She looked down at the close clover, wondering what was going to happen, leaving the two men to talk because she felt helpless and ignorant.

Bruce had opened suddenly like a flower on a palm-tree, meeting another man, one of the kind that Julie called book men. Blaize was carrying a typewriter that he had brought back from his father's. He was going to write seriously at last. But he was young. For two years he had been going to write. Yes, for two years he had lived really in the country, thinking a lot, reading a lot, lazing, gardening, wanting to be left alone, yet with an unsatisfied ache that kept biting at his content. She was perfectly sure that he would write seriously at last, because he had brought his typewriter. All the way across the common she saw genius oozing out of him.

The cottage, when it really came in sight, took their breath away, so that they could hardly say the real 'Oh!' they felt. It stood well back from the lane, at the bottom of a garden of luxuriant vegetation, potatoes and poppies, scarlet runners and sweet peas.

It was thatched, and had four windows, now tightly closed. Blaize had been away for a fortnight.

'I don't know what sort of a state it'll be in,' he said. 'We had to rush away for Sally's operation.'

He opened the door with a large key, and they waited in the garden, suddenly shy. Presently, he came out with three large, green-mouldy loaves in his arms, shouting, 'I don't know what to do with these. They've made a nasty mark on the tablecloth.'

He had got out of the bus at Salisbury, and bought new Salisbury bread, and butter, and jam. And soon he had a meal ready, and they all ate in love and friendliness.

He said, 'You can stay here if you like for a bit. It's lonely without Sally. I'll be very glad.'

But he could not find the sheets. However, there were some buff curtains, with thinnish bone rings at one end, and a camp bed. Quietly, with complete generosity, he gave up all his own things, the bedding from underneath and above him. But it was summer, and warm.

There was a ukulele hanging in a case from a beam, and Bruce took it down and began playing popular tunes of four or five years ago on it. Julie had not known that he could do this. It made her heart ache to think that for some unknown, youthful reason he had once spent strenuous hours learning to pluck notes from gut with his finger-ends. His face expressed intense concentration. For some time, he was not sure of himself, and played badly.

Blaize lifted the instrument out of his hands, and sang 'Early one morning', as if he had done it very many times before. It was his instrument; he knew it and was used to it. He crowed. But Bruce took it back and afterwards played softly and beautifully, making harmony out of the tinkling strings. The men mellowed and at the same time grew babylike, and Julie stood aside looking at their wise, momentarily innocent and empty eyes, herself surprised in another whirlwind of wisdom.

For the first time since their marriage, they slept in different beds. She went upstairs first, and took the camp bed greedily, because it had the softer mattress. Her head was low, and up near the open window. She blew out the candle, and moved so that she could look into the soft moist, country darkness. And presently, in spite of the noise from below, the laughter of the men and their deep voices booming through the wooden floor, she slept. Then she woke again. The voices were still going on, but more softly. Outside, the night was still quieter, and she thought that the world was looking up in pain and all the rest of the sky looking down in pity. Imagining perfection, she wept.

When Bruce came up, she relit the candle and watched him undress. He was so serious. All the talk, all the thought, all the laughter had been dismissed coming up the stairs. He took off a sock with a hole in it, looked at it very sadly, told her just where and when he had bought the socks, and how much he had paid for them. Her eyes knew him.

When he was ready for bed, he kneeled down and kissed her good morning. It was almost dawn. She wanted to say to him, 'I don't know anything. I can't talk to you. You'll always have to go to other people for talk. I'm only just beginning to know there are things.' But with his sound, satisfied touch on her shoulder, she forgot, and only murmured, 'Go to your bed'. His warm cheek was taken from hers reluctantly. She heard his bed creak, and thought to herself 'How it creaks, creaks'. And in a minute, it seemed, Blaize was at the door with tea and bread and eggs. He had got up early, and had been to the farm. They could hardly eat for bliss.

His room was filled with books. They ran about the wooden floor with bare feet, pulling a book out here and one there, pushing aside sacks of potatoes and papers spread with onions.

For two days they lived with Blaize chastely, talking, listening, playing shanties and Mozart and spirituals and rather old dance records on the gramophone. Always it seemed to be a meal-time. Blaize did all the work, slowly, so that it did not seem a penance, but a pleasant game.

'Who does the washing?'

'Oh, we do it.'

'That means Sally does it,' she thought. And a new, friendly feeling for Sally grew up in her mind. She had never met Sally, but she would know her, meet her, soon. Would Sally wash the buff curtains, with the white, sewn-on rings? And the pillow-slips, and the towels? Sally would be glad, must be glad for them. She dared not wonder why.

Again on the third day they went.

'You'll come back?'

'Of course we'll come back.'

The next bed was a feather bed. It was the landlady's own, and she gave it up to them. She was big and soft-voiced, and they liked her at once. Julie was happy because they were quite alone again. 'Aren't there a lot of lovely people in the world? Even Miss Lippincott. And Blaize and Sally' (he knew immediately what she meant) 'and now Mrs Wood.'

Bruce kept wanting to say 'How are you, Mrs Wood?'

After the landlady had prepared the feather bed, she sent her daughter in with supper. A glass of bitter, a pint of beer ('Thank God for the handle,' Bruce said — he liked his glass to have a handle), some cheese and a huge jar of home-pickled onions. They ate five each, silent with joy. The daughter was a nice girl, big and wide-waisted like her mother. She, too, had a gramophone, and kept putting on her favourite record:

> When are you going to lead to me the altar,
> Walter,
> When are you going to name the happy day?

The lamps were all on a level with their eyes, so that they stumbled about the unaccustomed passages and tripped up the narrow stairs.

'Shall we go for a little walk?'

'Yes.'

'We'll be in before eleven, Mrs Wood.'

An intense, steel-grey twilight had fallen over the quiet place. The small, decaying town was in a valley, and the downs rose on all sides like truculent shoulders. An incredibly tall, square church tower stood planted, for ever, it seemed, darkening the grey gloom with the shadow that its very age gave out. Except for the occasional sound of a spluttering motor cycle or car on the main road, the night was deeply still.

When the couple had climbed a hill and walked past a grey-walled farm to a new cross-road, they turned back and walked through a small wood, talking in low voices.

She said, 'This can't go on for ever.'

The girl had never known what it was to have a little money. She had always had to work for her living, and this honeymoon seemed to her to be closing as a fortnight's holiday should do.

'Why shouldn't it, darling?'

He was amused.

She could not find words to answer, but she sighed and tried to think of some way of convincing him that life must be taken firmly. That one played for so long, and then worked.

'We've got to find somewhere to live.'

'Of course. Let's take the first empty house we see.'

'What, here?'

'Yes.'

Her heart began to beat quickly. This is what comes of not knowing a man. This is what comes of marrying an income.

'Bruce, have you ever worked?'

'I have. For a whole year. But I didn't like it. And then my grandfather conveniently died.'

Of course, she had known all this, she had asked him these questions before, and he had patiently answered her. But a dreaminess began to grow over her, like the first beginnings of moss on a stone wall. There are people who don't have to fight for every penny. Now I am one of them. I didn't realize it. In the same moment she hated and loved the stranger by her side, and feared the thing she could not realize.

'You're not worrying, are you? You know there's enough for two of us to live on.'

'Of course I'm not. But you don't earn it. It'll be a different kind of money from any I've known. Listen to the trees.'

There was no wind at all, everything around was still, yet, high up, a small, murmuring leaf-noise could be heard.

'They're talking to us. Must be. There's nobody else about.' She could see the gleam of his teeth through the warm darkness, and for some reason began faintly to tremble, to look for glimpses of dark sky through the tree-tops, to escape from thought.

'My sweet, my love!'

When they reached the inn, it was late, and Julie felt guilty because of the warm and shining happiness which had routed thought and left only a bemused desire for sleep. 'Mrs Wood won't mind,' Bruce said, exerting himself enough to sprint down the last stretch of straight road. 'And we shall be in bed in five minutes.'

There had been a car break-down, and the inn was still brightly lit. For Mrs Wood had recently installed a petrol pump. She hovered about the car which would not go, full of goodwill and the knowledge of her petrol.

They said good night and closed their door behind them. Bruce lit a candle, and they examined their new room for the first time. It was full of presents from Weymouth, from Bournemouth, and from Poole. A small windmill had Marken on it. There were shell-sided boxes with glass-topped views, and wooden boxes with Weymouths and Bournemouths and Pooles on them in pokerwork. Bruce lifted a lid gingerly, and found a collection of childish handkerchiefs and coral necklaces and bracelets and other presents from Weymouth and Bournemouth and Poole. There was a large, framed photograph of a solemn, black-moustached man with letters an inch high beneath it, 'A Happy New Year from . . .'

'Marken must have a history all to itself.'

The night was warm, and the bed was warm, too, but they slept close and unmoving until after ten. Everything was leisurely. They ate in a tiny kitchen, and then had sandwiches packed, and walked over the downs all day long. There was a wind, and some light, thin showers. They walked for long stretches without speaking, dull under a dull sky. Grey-striped flies stung their arms, and each time they sat down to rest or eat, small, unknown insects bit their legs.

Julie was near tears. She had come upon a gap in the crowded days. Besides, all the rest of the times there had been sunshine. 'Does he feel like this, I wonder?' she asked herself.

She longed for her home, her mother and sisters, even her brothers. Bruce was alone, but for her, without mother or father, brother or sister, uncle or aunt. He was used to being alone. She forced back her tears and sat silently scratching herself. Bruce was finishing a sandwich at her side. She looked at his great dark head, his wide, fanatical brown eyes, his large-nostrilled nose, his eyebrows like chips of jet, his lips that looked hard and were surprisingly soft, and the thin but very definite line of his jaw, and wondered why she had once thought of him as 'that quiet boy', and had recalled his presence with an effort. 'Yes, you come, Bruce. Come with us,' and of how he had started willingly forward, just as he would have stayed willingly behind. And yet, all this had happened. His quietness that was as sure as anything on earth is sure. His certainty and her mercurial nature together. The things he thought, and the things she thought! Yet occasionally they were the same.

That night, they talked for a long time. They could not sleep. She lay high on the pillow, her hand under his arm, his head on the satiny plain of her breast. The clouds had drifted away with the sunset, and a silver, almost full, moon was rising, dimming their yellow and still-burning candle.

All their talk was foolish talk; snatches of past days. Now and then they hurt each other, trying to sting as the flies had stung them throughout the day. Under their backs, the feather bed grew warmer and warmer.

'Let's go out.'

'How dare we?'

'What do you mean, "How dare we?" Who's to stop us?'

'Well, I mean, how do we get out and back?'

He was already half-dressed. 'Through the door, of course.'

She had to beat back the words from her lips, as she realized she would always have to beat them back and follow the man silently.

She put on her clothes. There was the responsibility of leaving the inn door open. Why didn't Bruce think it was important? There was the fact that if they were not back by early morning, Mrs Wood would think the strangest things.

'Quietly.'

Before he blew out the candle flame, he looked over his shoulder and laughed. She laughed and took his hand, and they crept downstairs together, their blood in perfect rhythm. The house was very old, and creaked and groaned in its troubled sleep. The air was chill outside. For a time, past all the houses, they walked on tiptoe.

'Where are we going?' She looked up at his face, pale and austere and once again inexplicably dear in the moonlight. They were now walking on a white lane between two hedges.

'We're going to see the giant in the moonlight.'

On the hillside in front of them was a great figure cut from the chalky ground. Upheld in his right hand was a huge club. His face looked small and round and far-away.

'We're going to climb to the top of the hill.'

'Yes,' she said contentedly.

But it was hard to find the way, and she feared the treacherous moonlight. 'Bull, bulls,' she kept thinking; and she saw illustrations in magazines of enormous, snorting bulls running after people who had no earthly chance of escaping from them. Bruce walked in front of her, looking for some kind of a track, and she plodded behind him, conscious of every hillock, of every bush or stone that might move and prove itself to be a bull. But gradually something in the cool and moonlit night took hold of her and overcame her fear.

They were almost breathless from rapid, purposeful movement when at last they reached the face of the giant. They looked at what could be seen of the sleeping village on their left, the dark trees, the square tower of the church which now seemed to be no longer Christian, but sheer pagan.

'Come here.'

She came willingly, and sat down with her husband on a raised nostril of the friendly giant. First the hill seemed large to her, then the country, and the sea surrounding it. She thought of high hills, of Alps and Himalayas and Andes, and then again of this place where two humans sat under the moon; this hill not more filled with secrets than any other hill, but holding evidence of other lives that had been lived here long before them.

She sat for a long time, near her husband and yet apart, looking into the night silently. But first her small vexations had to go; the open inn door, the candle-grease that Bruce had spilt on the pillow, her own vague longing for home and the life she had formerly known.

She felt peace inside herself at last. Had she been brought here to learn of this gracious silence from the night? To accept life as this hill accepted time? For how many thousand years had the man-carved giant shaken his defiant club at the sky? Nobody knew. Tomorrow he might be gone, broken in bits by some freak volcanic upheaval, even sunk to the bottom of the sea. It did not matter. Some new man would make some new wonder on some new hill.

She wanted to break a piece from this enchanted night and send it down the ages; but there was nothing to take. There was only the thought of the down that billowed around them, the darkly silvered trees in the valley, the shut and sheltered houses, the solemn ecstasy of the moonlight, the ebb and flow of the near and distant sea; and that thought would go on.

Within an hour they were back at the inn again, and asleep. Their faces were calm, smooth, and unshadowed. And at that instant, not even Time himself could have guessed with what lines they would be engraved when he had finished with them.

Strange Music

THE TWO young girls trudged along through the rain and wind, their waterproof capes, a gay blue and a gayer red, flapping around them. Joyce, the taller of the two, kept her face up to the storm, but Cora, the small dark one, bent under it, shrinking from the gusts and the spattering wetness.

'We oughtn't to have come, really,' said the latter in a tone so low that her taller friend had to stoop to listen. 'He mightn't be playing there tonight, he only said perhaps he would. And his wife might have turned up. She often does.'

'And pigs might fly,' comforted Joyce, in the cheerful voice of one without a care in the world. 'He'll be there all right, alone.'

'Oh, Joyce, you do say the most lovely things. I wonder if that's why I like you so much. You seem to say just what I'm always hoping.'

'Mind you,' Joyce shouted against a miniature gale, 'I think we're being a bit silly, and I don't think he's worth a lift of your little finger, but I know you can't go for long without seeing him. Is this the place?'

'Oh, no, not yet. It's quite a long way. I told you. And I hope you don't mind. But I do feel, seeing we've come so far, we might as well go right on to the end.'

'Hm, that's always been your way. Perhaps if you'd stopped before the end with him, you mightn't feel the way you do.'

'Well, I didn't,' said Cora, pulling with difficulty a handkerchief from an undercoat pocket and wiping her wet face. 'I couldn't. And if it all came over again, I shouldn't do anything but just what I have done, even if it has left me liking him more than he likes me.'

'Liking?' scoffed her friend, blinking up into the darkness of the night.

'Well, loving, then. We turn up this street. And it was my fault. We all know when to stop, and I didn't. But it has made everything seem different. I'm not going to dance, I don't feel like it.'

'Not going to dance? Well, you don't mind if I have just one, do you? I can't hear a band without my feet going. What about his wife?'

'Of course have one,' Cora smiled. 'It'll give me a chance to talk to him — if he's there. His wife's nice. He likes her a lot. And she really looks after him well. It makes me feel sort of — grateful.'

It was early — not yet half past nine — when the girls entered the dance hall ante-room, and the quietness was nearly that of the grave. One subdued light burned above an array of wooden chairs, which waited as if for a ghostly audience. A flight of stairs started, thinning as it branched into two parts where it struck the wall. Opposite the stairway, two doors led into a brightly lit ballroom, at the far end of which six neat young men on a raised platform waited for the signal to strike up their music.

The drum had the words Danny Dunne painted across it, and a placard saying Danny Dunne also hung from the cream-coloured concert grand. As the girls peered through a bright doorway, their eyes confused by the sharp light, a seventh young man, graceful and good-looking, ran lightly to the front, whispered something into a microphone, which converted his whisper into a growling roar, turned round, and appeared to galvanize his meagre band into immediate life.

'He's here. Danny's here,' said Cora, watching the elegant back with fevered eyes.

Joyce looked wonderingly down on her friend, and said, 'I don't really know what you see in him. His clothes look nice, and he's clever, but — '

Cora turned and gave the other girl a long, female look. They laughed together, a little hysterically. They were alone in the ante-room, except for a dull-looking group of men in dark lounge suits talking together. On the left was a paybox. The women inside it had not noticed the entry of the two girls. They had paid nothing.

'Put your cloak and rubber shoes down here, Joyce, and go in for your dance,' said Cora urgently, 'and then when the interval comes, tell Danny I'm here. Tell him I'm only here for a minute, I have to be home by ten.' Her face was flushed and her eyes were bright with the glimpse she had had of the young man. 'And don't let anybody see you.'

A gay howl of sound and an intermittent shuffling of feet came from beyond the two lighted doorways. Joyce had sailed in and got a partner immediately. She always did, wherever she went, even if she had to kidnap him temporarily. Nobody could withstand that bright, proprietary air, that calmly joyous body, that wide-toothed smile. And she could dance well, though she always wanted to pull her partner her way instead of being led.

Cora turned and looked at the stairs, the dim light, the girl in the paybox, who was chewing something rhythmically and reading a paper-backed novel; there was nothing else to be seen. The dark-suited group of men had melted away in some unnoticed moment. Then five or six shiny-haired youths clattered down the stairs from a balcony above, and stood around sheepishly, not wanting to enter the ballroom until the music had finished. They kept giving way to bursts of raucous laughter.

Cora's heart began to beat with dread. She always feared that somebody might speak to her, and that she would not know what to say, and that she might one day even be struck or beaten in some brawl which had sprung up outside her knowledge.

And all at once the music stopped, as quick as that. There would be no encore, there were not enough dancers on the floor for Danny to bother with so difficult a number.

But it started up again immediately, and the girl resigned herself to a longer wait, her hand clutching her gloves and bag to her wet raincape. A strand of curled wet hair hung down her forehead under the scarlet hood. She turned as she heard footsteps, unable to believe that the young man she had come to see was standing in front of her.

'Hullo,' he said awkwardly, holding out his hand.

'Hullo,' she said. She could only stare at the studs in his shirt. 'Your studs are nice.'

His untaken hand moved towards them, self-consciously, and he smiled. There was a long silence.

'What made you turn up?' he asked. There was a sudden crescendo in the music.

'To see you,' she said humbly. They blushed.

'Cora,' he said softly. 'You shouldn't. You mustn't. You know it isn't —' He could not find the words he wanted to say, and stood there uneasily, young, unhappy, trapped.

'I can't help it,' she said in a stubborn voice. 'And there's nothing you need do. All I want is to see you now and again. Only I have to come to see you now instead of you coming to see me. That's the only difference.'

'I'm sorry, Cora.'

'That's all right.' She laughed. 'Your studs *are* nice, you know,' she said in a more natural voice, 'I've never seen you working before. Fancy that! When I looked in at the door and saw you up there on the platform, you could have struck me down with a feather, really you could. I've never seen you in this suit.' She put out her hand and began to stroke his soft black sleeve. He gave a sharp look at the unheeding woman in the paybox, and then stood still under her caress, staring helplessly before him.

'Danny,' her voice was urgent. 'I want to see you again. I do. I want us to be alone again together. You know what I want. You to be there, and not anybody else in the world. You know how it is, Danny.' Her hand left his sleeve, and slipped slowly, softly, down the side of his coat.

'Don't,' he said. 'Not here. Anybody might see us. I've got to be careful.' His large eyes looked enormous in the gloom. He moved back a step, and the light hand fell away from his coat.

'Everything's all right for you,' she said in a conversational tone. 'You're a man, you can get away with anything. But here I am, I had to come. What on earth do you think brought me? It's simply that I can't help it. It's as if you had got me on a piece of string, ever since that first time, and you wouldn't let go your end. I would,' she went on, 'I'd let go, if I were able to. Will you let me go?'

'I don't know what you mean.'

'Oh, yes, you do. You know what I mean all right. Everything could end now — our meeting each other, I mean, and being ashamed. Not the other. Nothing could end that. It'll go on for ever and ever, and when I'm dead I'll come back for you.' She laughed. 'I shall die first, you know, and perhaps you'll forget me for a while, and I shall not trouble you at all, but when you die, you'll remember. "She'll be waiting," and what will you think then? I love you, Danny,' she said in a rapid whisper, 'I love you and I love you and I love you. Now will you let me go?'

'I still don't know what you mean.' With one ear he was listening to his band. Here was where he should have picked up his violin and played solo. The music sounded thin without his accompanying melody.

'Yes, you do know what I mean. If you really didn't want me I could get away from you. Do you think it's any pleasure to know you're chained to someone?' She was speaking more angrily now. 'I've said it over and over again. Will you let me go?'

He looked at her for a long time. It seemed *now* for a long time. His eyelids flickered, and for a moment he was drained and old. Then he said. 'No, I don't want you to go.'

A flame shot through the girl, and roared above her head. The dim electric globe flickered. The paybox girl turned a page of her novel, and the light above her touched a bulge in her cheek as she rolled the toffee in her mouth. The stairs stood like Atlas, with branching arms, holding a weight almost too great to be borne, and the music suddenly blared brassily, nearing its end.

'Well, there it is,' said the girl easily, 'I suppose that means you have a bit of love for me.'

'I suppose it does.'

They stood apart in the dim light, listening to the shuffling feet and the scattered applause.

'Joyce'll be back in a minute. We're not staying. I love you, I love you. Don't forget.'

'No. I'll have to get back for the next number.'

'I love you. Of course you will. Here's Joyce. We're going, you know. Joyce has sneaked that dance. We've not paid, and we're not going to, now. It was nice seeing you, Danny.'

'I enjoyed myself,' said Joyce, turning towards her and laughing. 'But you'd better go back, Danny. Everything falls to bits without you.'

The young man smiled, and shook hands conventionally with the two girls. Cora watched him go through the doorway, and gave a shuddering sigh.

'Well, are you ready?' Joyce asked, a little sternly.

'Yes.'

The wind battered them as they stepped outside the dance hall door.

'You seemed to have plenty to say to him,' said Joyce. 'Was his wife there?'

'I don't know. I never asked him.'

They turned the corner into the main road. The rain glistened on the uneven surface of the dark highway, and the wind made rippling waves form on the shallow pools.

'We shall have to hurry to catch the ten o'clock bus. Have you arranged to meet him, again?'

'No, I haven't,' Cora said.

There was some strange music in her head, and she was listening to it. It wasn't dance music — it wasn't easy music at all. It was slow-beating and grave, already like a funeral march heard afar off, and had nothing whatever to do with her youth, or her body which battled against the twisting wind. The tall friend put a hand on her arm to help her along, and shouted some words in a laughing voice to a passer-by, but she hardly heard them because of the strong, sad, remembered music which was flooding her being.

(This story was first published in *Lilliput*, July 1940.)

Time for Chapel

PATIENCE was met at the door by Aunt Florida, now seventy, and by the remembered ⸗mell of polished oilcloth.

She looked, not at Aunt Florida's unsmiling face, but at the steep, light-brown painted stairs and their respectable red carpet, protected in its turn by a foot-wide covering of well-washed near-linen, which ran up behind the old woman like a photographer's back-cloth. The hall was merely this box-like entrance. The kitchen lay on one side of it, and the parlour on the other.

'So ye had to come in a taxi?' said the aunt, looking over her niece's head at the driver, who, in the lane at the bottom of the long garden, was trying to turn his car in the roadway's narrow space.

'How else could I come, Aunt?' said Patience with a timid smile. 'You wouldn't expect me to walk at my age, would you?'

'The trams don't run any longer, but a bus passes the chapel now, and that's only a five-minutes' walk. But perhaps London's taken the goodness out of your feet?' She looked Patience over critically. 'Ye needn't have bedizened your face for me. I don't like it. However, come in.'

Patience could have cried. Even at thirty-eight she was as much a stranger to, and as much afraid of, Aunt Florida as she had been at the age of eight. Afraid of those black, beady and almost unwinking eyes that stared into the middle of her tiny soul and knew it for what it was.

She stumbled up the three stone steps, over the brown mat which slipped under her feet, and into the large and spotless kitchen with its great blackleaded range, its shining steel fender, and its stiff wooden chairs that stood as straight as ramrods. The front half of the table, she was glad to see, was laid for tea, over the red plush cloth with the dustless tassels — the same cloth that she had had to shake twice a day on the square of lawn in her far-off childish days.

'You can have Uncle Pulteney's room. And wash your face and keep it washed while you stay with me. There's no need for that muckment here. And pull yourself together. Do you think you're the first woman whose husband has left her?'

Patience began to sniff uncontrollably, and the tears splashed down her cheeks on to her smart blue suit. Through them, she saw her plump hands, with their soft, useless palms and nicely-kept fingernails.

'Well,' she said, 'he has left me with enough money to live on.'

'Tcha!' returned her aunt. 'Be quick. The kettle's boiling. Don't keep me waiting.'

Patience went upstairs into the bedroom over the parlour. It was no different. The suite of bird's-eye maple with the imitation Tudor bed was still there, every piece in its accustomed place, the dressing-table in front of the double window, the high chest of drawers a yard away from the bed, the unused washstand to the right of the door, and the wardrobe to the right of the window. Still there were the two pictures of young girls, one with her arms full of fruit, one holding nothing — the greedy and the good, she used to call them, liking neither — and the gilt fire-screen with its blue and green peacock at display.

Patience put down her case, took off her hat and coat, washed hurriedly in the neat bathroom, and went down to tea. Since leaving London, she had hardly dared to stop and think for a minute of the comfortable house she had shared with her husband Charles, the limitless supply of drinks, the theatres and cinemas, the aimless existence, the laxity of life. She had had fifteen years of it. There must be some change in her.

Aunt Florida's teacups were ugly, high and wide, with a looped gold band an inch from the top. But they and the plates shone. All the food was on hand-crocheted doilies, and the bread and cakes were home made. Patience remembered everything. But it had not seemed the same when she was young.

Oh, how stifling she had found it then! How she had longed to get away from Aunt Florida's strictness, from the routine, even from the excessive cleanliness. Everything must be done just so. Soap must never come near the teacups. They must be washed in water almost boiling, and dried on a cloth that was perfectly clean. The dish cloths — one for the washing up and one for the stone sink — must be hung outside on the line near the scullery door. The whole house must be swept and polished every day.

Why, why, she had wondered, sulkily and rebelliously, why must I do all this? Work all the week long, and chapel three times on Sunday? All the same, there had been the lovely surprises, the stolen walks over the moorway — it wasn't exactly a moor, but all that was left of one — looking for four-leaved clovers, when a five-minutes' giggling chat with a neighbour's boy had seemed like a three-volume romance, and the absorbing topic of a new straw hat had filled weeks of time.

'What are ye thinking of doing next?' Her aunt's voice cut into her thoughts. The old woman still wore the high-necked blouses and wide black skirts of her remembered youth. Her grey-black hair was drawn into the same tight knob at the back of her neck, and her skin's yellowing folds were deeper. She wore gold-rimmed eye-glasses for reading only, and now they hung from a ribbon pinned to her dress and swayed as she spoke.

Patience had wondered that many times herself. But after the first shock, and the knowledge that her husband would never return to her — he had, in fact, run off with the woman who had called herself Patience's friend — she had simply wanted to go back to her childhood's home, and the only home she remembered was her Aunt Florida's.

'I don't know.' She was forcing herself to eat, because she did not want any comments from her aunt.

'Well, you've got to do something,' said the old woman in her hard voice. 'Satan finds some mischief still — you know the rest.'

'I told you before that Charles has left me enough money. I can go back and live the same way I've done for the last fifteen years, only without him.' She lifted her large cup of tea in a trembling hand and tried to drink.

'That's grand sort of money to use,' said her aunt sarcastically, 'and much good it's done you. Get up!' she said suddenly and fiercely. 'Get up and look in the glass, and see what it's done for you already! Have you ever had a thought outside of yourself! Have you ever done a hand's turn for anyone else? Look at your shilly-shallying face, look at your dolly hands. You can spend your time in manicuring them, but what do you do with them, besides putting food into your mouth? Tcha! I'm ashamed to think I brought you up!'

'I can go,' said Patience, crying helplessly, 'I can go.' She had not looked in the mirror, knowing only too well what she would see there — the large, plaintive eyes, the softly waved brown hair, the moist, drooping lips, the snub nose that had been so adorable when she was eighteen. Oh, why had she come here to be treated like this? She had written to her aunt with full particulars of her troubles, and had come back thinking that this time the old woman would unbend, that she would condemn Charles and give the badly treated wife sympathy, and perhaps even affection. And all she got was this.

'We can't all be perfect,' she went on, wiping her red eyelids. 'Like *you*.'

'Perfect!' snorted her Aunt. 'Perfect? I'm doing the work I have to do from morning to night — and perhaps in ten more years, if I'm alive, I might be able to tell you why. I certainly don't know now. I might have been like you when your uncle left me, but I've changed, I've changed.'

'When Uncle left you?' gasped Patience, forgetting to cry. 'But Uncle was always here.'

'Oh, yes he came home to die. And he took a long, long time to do it. Now take the tea-things into the scullery and wash them. And remember how I like to have things done. And then we will play cribbage.'

Patience went to a well-remembered drawer, and took out a stiffly-starched apron. By the time her aunt had come down again, she had drawn up the card-table — which was a wooden one, made by her sailor grandfather, and marked with brown and yellow squares for either chess or draughts — and got out the cribbage board from behind the sewing machine. The two of them played, at first almost silently, than, after a marking error, with a kind of noisy politeness. 'Fifteen two, fifteen four, fifteen six, seven eight nine ten, eleven twelve, thirteen fourteen. That's a lucky run — lucky for me the six turned up. Ha — and two for a pair make sixteen.'

After supper, they shared the work, raked out the dying fire, and went to bed. Aunt Florida's parting words were, 'Don't forget, it's Sunday tomorrow and chapel's at half-past ten.'

For a long time the younger woman could not sleep. Before going to bed, she stood looking at herself in the long mirror, the candle in its brass candlestick held high above her head. She had seen for the first time the futile vacancy of her look, the look of a woman who, as her aunt used to say, knows nothing and cares less.

At the beginning of her married life, she had cared something. She was sure she loved her husband, and let herself be led by him. 'Yes, Charles,' and 'No, Charles,' she would say, as he wished. He could earn money, but he could spend it, too. She could not keep up with him, and bit by bit dropped her exhausted hold. It was more easy to sit at home and just do nothing, or go to a comforting play or film than really dress and be polite and nice to his friends. She excused herself over and over again. She would even have liked a baby or two, not because of a deep love of human life, but simply to have had something to play with for a few years, but Charles didn't like or want children, so of course she had done without. And now, that part of her life was over.

What had been her aunt's last words before her 'good night'? 'Sunday tomorrow. Chapel. Half-past ten.'

She began to think about chapel. All it had once meant to her was sitting uncomfortably on a wooden bench, seeing the various new hats and coats of the congregation; listening to Miriam Chapelow's piercing soprano voice in the choir, smelling mothballs and the sweetish odour of new crêpe, moving about and coughing if the preacher went on too long, and coming home to a tea in which stewed prunes and a new sandwich cake took the leading parts.

What would chapel be like now? There would be people to meet — after fifteen years spent in London, she still knew nearly everybody in the northern village — and they all liked to gossip and to know things. They would be curious about her life in London, and her husband. (How had Aunt Florida behaved when Uncle had left her?) They would comment on Charles, and wonder why she came so rarely to see her aunt. 'She won't always be as healthy as she is now. Someone ought to be living with her,' they would say.

She shivered, and pulled the sheet more closely round her neck. She had drawn up the blind, and could see the dressing-table darkly in the large square of window light, with its horn-shaped hair-tidy hanging from the mirror's upright arm, and the three mats on which stood the lavender water, the brush and comb plate, and the round pin-box which she knew had a picture of a solitary violet on its lid. How could it be, she wondered, that all these things stayed the same, while her own house had crumbled about her, like an earthen cliff under a too stormy sea?

But soon the silence of the night brought her thoughts to a halt, and she slept. At eight o'clock, there was a rap on her door. She woke to a blaze of sunlight.

'What is it?' she called, still half asleep.

'Get up,' came her aunt's voice through the closed door. 'It's enough for you to have your Uncle Pulteney's room without lying in it all day.'

When Patience got downstairs, the old woman was sitting bolt upright beside the window, reading her Bible. There was a bright fire, the hearth was cleaned, and breakfast was laid, with bread and butter, egg-cups, and marmalade in a glass jar which caught and reflected the shafts of morning sunlight in its facets.

'I have done the work today,' said Aunt Florida, looking through her gold-rimmed glasses. 'But you can come down at seven tomorrow. We will take turns. It will be a rest for me.'

'Yes, Aunt,' said Patience. She felt this morning as if a little of youth had been returned to her as a gift, and she wished to turn it over and over.

' "Thus saith the Lord," her aunt read aloud. "Cursed be the man that trusteth in man, and maketh flesh his arm, and whose heart departeth from the Lord.

' "For he shall be like the heath in the desert, and shall not see when good cometh; but shall inhabit the parched places in the wilderness, in a salt land and not inhabited.

' "Blessed is the man that trusteth the Lord, and whose hope the Lord is.

' "For he shall be as a tree planted by the waters, and that spreadeth out her roots by the river, and shall not see when heat cometh, but her leaf shall be green; and shall not be careful in the year of drought, neither shall cease from yielding fruit."

'Take the eggs off,' she went on in the same tone of voice.

'They've been on four minutes. And brew the tea.'

'Yes, Aunt,' said Patience, obediently.

Of her own accord, she rose immediately the meal was over, and did the household chores, and knew that she was doing them well and that her aunt would approve. And all the time, she was thinking of the words the old woman had been reading, and remembering how her aunt would always read from her Bible before breakfast, and how she had laughed in her heart in those years gone by, and thought of all the things she would get from life without the aid of a Bible. And how those years had passed, and she had got nothing. And of the fear and emptiness that had pulled her home.

As she straightened her sheets, she began to think more painfully, not about herself and her troubles, but of other people. She wondered for the first time about her husband, and what he really wanted, what he needed and had not been given by life. He had always been elusive — had put off her questions with a laugh or a light caress. She had never been bad-tempered, but just flabby. Not once had she felt anger. Even at the last, she had only cried and cried, and agreed to everything he said. Had she been simply a doormat?

And why had she come back to Aunt Florida? There were other people to whom she could have gone for consolation — and got it. Oh, yes, she had her friends, friends who would have liked her money, and not thrown the very thought of it back in her teeth, as Aunt Florida had thrown it. But the old woman was straightforward, she was strength in a world of weakness. But no, she must not say that. 'Cursed be the man that trusteth in man, and maketh flesh his arm, and whose heart departeth from the Lord.'

She sat down in the cane-bottomed chair and thought again about chapel. From very far down, she began to remember how she had felt in her teens, how she had gone about looking for something to worship, and had never found anything. Oh, but how she had tried! How fervently she had sung the hymns, and closed her eyes during silent prayer. And how glad she felt that she had dimly understood something when old, crippled Mrs Horncastle had embroidered a cloth with the words:

Lord of Harvest, grant that we
Wholesome grain and pure may be

to be used at Harvest Festival. Yes, there had been something really satisfying about chapel. People in their Sunday clothes and under the roof of God had been a little kinder than they were outside for a little while. They meant well, however badly they behaved once the chapel doors had closed behind them.

The rest of her life dropped from her mind, and she could think only of chapel. Of the visiting parsons, and how they would thunder and denounce. Heaven was real, and hell was real, and there was none of this shabby half-and-half business, where nothing really happened, and where husbands left their wives, not for a great and perfect love, but for something exceedingly like that which they were leaving. They were making flesh their arm, that was all.

She was still sitting in her chair when her aunt entered the room dressed in her Sunday best.

'Do you know it is twenty past ten?' she said icily, 'and chapel starts at half past.'

'I'm not going,' said Patience.

'You're not going?' repeated her aunt.

'No, I'm not,' she said stubbornly, looking at the old woman, taking in her gaunt figure, her almost military black coat, her proud mien, her calm, folded lips and sure eyes, remembering her own image in the mirror, and wondering for a flickering instant if her indeterminate face could ever be so moulded by the years.

'Please yourself,' said her aunt in a low voice. She went over to the window, straightened a blind, walked back a few steps, leaned over, and kissed her niece's forehead with unpractised lips.

'Not now, perhaps,' she continued in the same low voice; 'not this week, nor next, even. But you'll come to it, you'll come.'

She clutched her things more tightly, the rolled black umbrella, the one kid glove which she had pulled off to straighten the blind, the black handbag which held a handkerchief and her peppermints and her collection money and nothing more, and turned and walked out of the bedroom.

No Stone for Jochebed

AFTER she was perfectly sure that this time Cousin Jochebed had really done what she had so often threatened to do, and died, Mrs Ebthwaite covered up the sharp, mean little face on the white pillow and walked ponderously downstairs.

'She's gone, Luke,' she said to the sandy little man who was sitting with his stockinged feet on the fender, his coat draped behind him on the wooden chair-back, reading the evening paper. 'She's gone at last.'

Luke Ebthwaite gave her a cautious, serious glance, rubbed his hand over his tufty ginger hair, and waited to hear what his instructions were to be. But the woman hesitated and frowned, setting her mouth in a grim, unpleasant line, and did not seem to be certain of her next move.

'Did she say anything?' asked the little man.

'Aye, she said a lot,' his wife returned. But she did not enlighten him at all. 'You'd better stop in while I fetch Mrs Ulper to lay her out. And I'll go over to our Clarry's to see what arrangements to make.'

'You'll what?' asked her husband, quite stupefied. It was not six months since he had stumped out of our Clarry's house behind his incensed wife, after trying his first and last bit of ineffectual peacemaking, and heard her say that she would never enter her sister's door again.

'You heard what I said. Clarry's my only sister, isn't she? And Jochebed was all the cousin we'd got between us.'

'Yes, but don't you remember all the things Clarry said the last time you went, about you plotting and planning, and stealing Jochebed right from under her nose? And how she threw Great-Aunt Maria's pot dog at me when I was pushing the handcart, and it broke by the wheel and she said she'd prosecute me?' protested the bewildered Luke, putting down his paper and beginning to light a brown, curly pipe which he drew warm from his trousers pocket.

'I remember that poor Jochebed's dead, and that there's a buryin' to go on with,' returned his wife, lifting her embedded chin to fasten a bit of fur round her thickish neck, looking into the mirror with the truculent expression with which she always looked into mirrors. 'And how many times have I told you, if you want to smoke your dirty pipe, go somewhere else to do it; don't stay in my clean kitchen.'

With the look of a martyr, the little man returned the pipe to his pocket. It would not be long before his wife was gone, then he could do as he liked — for a few minutes, anyhow.

Mrs Ebthwaite picked up her umbrella and opened the door. There was slight, fine rain. She walked down the four stone steps and the stone-flagged path to the gate. It was a dull, cool summer evening, and there were very few people about. Mr Leaf, who kept a general store which was also a Post Office, peeped through the window at his neighbour and felt moderately certain that something had happened to Cousin Jochebed at last.

This Cousin Jochebed had always been a hard-working woman, and it was known that she had saved two hundred pounds, and that it was to be left to whichever one of her cousins treated her the best. For years she had traded on this, and had lived first with one sister and then with the other, going off to her work every morning — she was a forewoman in a bookbindery — carrying a brown-paper parcel filled with a substantial lunch. She was a very small woman, yet she had a tremendous appetite, and was never done complaining that first one sister and then the other starved her to within an inch of her life. After a few weeks of living with Clarry, she would be off to Lyddie and Luke; then she would grow restless and go back to Clarry.

But six months ago things had come to a head. Clarry had put up some fish paste sandwiches for her lunch that she swore both tasted and smelt queer. ('Well, why did you eat them, then?' Clarry had asked in the course of the now historic quarrel that had followed.) She had come home and had been very ill. She had sent for Lyddie — 'and tell her to bring Luke and a handcart,' she had added. She usually left her larger belongings behind when she went from Clarry to Lyddie, but this time she took them with her, crying out dramatically that all was over, and they need never expect to see one penny of her money.

Inglehearn Bean, Clarry's husband, had not spoken a word to her for three days, because he was so angry and upset. He loved money more than anything else in the world, and had wanted Cousin Jochebed's two hundred pounds to come to Clarry just for the pleasure of taking it from her. He would never spend a penny where a ha'penny would do, as the saying is. Whatever his wife got or saved, he took to himself. She let it go, knowing it would be in even safer hands than hers. Yet he loved to see other people wasting money. Perhaps he felt that the more quickly they spent it, the more quickly it might come back to him. Clarry would save. The love of money ran through her family too, though the rumour was not true that she had tried to poison Jochebed with her fish paste sandwiches. She had never once thought of it.

When Lyddie Ebthwaite had seen Mrs Ulper and given her all instructions, she went next to her sister. Mr Leaf, still peering through the window, had expected her to make a bee-line for the undertaker's, but she had passed his house and gone straight down Minney Lane to where the Beans lived.

'Well, Clarry, I expect you're surprised to see me,' said Lyddie, closing her umbrella and putting her foot squarely into the landing in case her sister should have a mind to shut the door, 'but the truth is, Cousin Jochebed's gone at last, and I thought it only right to come and tell you.'

'Very nice of you, I'm sure,' said Clarry, sniffing. 'But come in — though I seem to remember you promising you'd never come into my house again.'

'Threatening, Clarry, threatening. And I had to do it for Jochebed's sake, the poor thing. She took on so about those sandwiches.'

Mrs Bean looked at her sister speechlessly, while her husband, Inglehearn — who was called England by everybody in the village, as his own name was so difficult — gave her an acid smile.

'Welcome once more, Lyddie,' he said, his nostrils twitching. 'It's very nice of you to come down and gloat over us, I'm sure, now that you've got everything you want.'

'I didn't come here to gloat over you, England,' said Lyddie, looking at her brother-in-law's dome-like head and large, grey

moustache, and thinking how much she disliked him. 'I really
came along for some advice about the funeral. What do you think
we ought to do about it?'

'How do you mean, what we ought to do?'

'I mean about the funeral. How many ought we to ask, and what
sort of a funeral do you think it's best to have?'

England thought rapidly. There was something astonishing
about Lyddie coming to him for advice, though it must be little
enough of advice or anything else that she could get out of Luke
Ebthwaite. Advice was cheap enough. It cost nothing.

'I think Cousin Jochebed ought to have a real, slap-up funeral,'
he pronounced. 'After all, who can afford it better than her?' He
sniggered, watching his sister-in-law flush dully almost down to
her wrists.

'If you think that, then it ought to be done,' said Lyddie after a
pause. This was so far from what they expected to hear that
England and Clarry looked at her with their mouths open.

'Yes, it ought to be done,' she repeated. Then, 'I wonder if
England will come along with me to Neville Crossley's,' she asked.
Neville Crossley was the village undertaker.

'Of course I will,' said England, already pressing his bowler hat
over his brow. 'But remember,' he said, archly, looking at her with
his bloodshot eyes, 'all expenses will have to come out of the two
hundred pounds, tee-hee.'

'If they have to, they have to,' said his sister-in-law, shortly. She
did not seem to like being reminded of the money.

The prospect before England caused him intense delight. He
whistled *The Miller of Dee* as he walked along beside Lyddie, trying
to dodge the spokes of her umbrella, and said, 'How do, Nev?' to
Mr Crossley, with more than a trace of levity. Mr Crossley was not
used to this kind of behaviour in the more delicate side of his
business. He had another department where he took orders for
coal, and where a joke or two now and then did not matter.

'Good evening,' he answered, rebukingly, and then in softer
tones to Lyddie, 'I suppose I am right in assuming that poor Miss'
— he had been in the village only twenty-four years and had not
had the pleasure of knowing the deceased's surname — 'your poor
cousin has passed away.'

'Yes, that's right,' returned Lyddie, shortly. 'England will see you about the expense. It's all to be paid for with Jochebed's money, as he'll probably tell you more than once. As far as I'm concerned,' she said, giving him a straight look, 'you can give her the best of what you've got — always bearing in mind that it's only two hundred pounds she's left,' she added, sarcastically. 'And now do you mind if I go home? I've a lot to attend to. Do you think you and Clarry might see about the invitations, too? Poor Jochebed had a lot of friends, and I'm sure she'd like them all to come. She talked a lot to me this afternoon, and said she'd like everybody to have a pair of black kid gloves, and that she wanted plenty of flowers, and I told her I'd do my very best to see that she got what she wanted.'

Mr Crossley's eyes brightened a good deal as he listened politely to Mrs Ebthwaite. Here was what he called a real order, and one which he could carry out with melancholy satisfaction. There was too much repression in his life as a general rule. He had never dared to branch out into the sort of funeral he really wanted.

It was quite dark before England Bean got home to his house in Minney Lane, and he was still whistling *The Miller of Dee* between his teeth. He kept on waking during the night and nudging Clarry in the side to remind her of something fresh he had thought of. 'There'll not be a fat lot of Jochebed's money left for your Lyddie and that henpecked husband of hers when I've finished ordering,' he chuckled. 'This is going to be a funeral they'll all remember. I've asked every man, woman and child in the place. There'll be twenty cabs if there's one. I've even got Ted Musto to play the organ. We're having music with it!'

No such funeral as Cousin Jochebed's had ever been seen before in this particular part of the country. In addition to the kid gloves, there was a crepe-bordered handkerchief for everyone — large for the men, medium for the women, and small for the children. A gardener in the next village, who raised hothouse flowers for the town market, brought over a lorryful of blooms.

Neville Crossley borrowed every cab he could lay his hands on, though there was hardly a quarter of a mile for anyone to ride, as the churchyard was only at the other end of the village. The vicar shook his head sadly, and thought unutterable thoughts, but said little beyond the words of the burial service. And underneath all, there was an air of suppressed excitement. The sisters and their husbands rode together in the first cab, as neither one of them would give way to the other, all of them dutifully holding the black-bordered handkerchiefs to their faces now and then for the edification of passing strangers.

And after Cousin Jochebed had been put away, what a feast they all went back to! The village hall had been hired, and half-a-dozen women, with Mrs Ulper at the head of them, were waiting with ham and tongue and pies and pastries and baked meats for the return of the funeral party.

For days, Luke Ebthwaite had been in a state of silent astonishment. At first, he had sat rubbing his ginger head and following his wife's every movement with his wondering little eyes. He had watched her absent-mindedly go into the scullery to wash the dirty dishes, and in her absent-mindedness even dry them — a job which always fell on him. He had taken out his curly pipe once or twice, and struck a match diffidently — she had never been able to stop his using matches instead of strips of newspaper; they were his one remaining stronghold — but she had taken not the least notice. So he had progressed from a surreptitious puff or two to whole sessions of smoking, and she had never said a word.

He couldn't help chuckling to himself at times over the whole business of Cousin Jochebed and her money. He didn't care a rap for the money, and had told her that she could leave it to the missionaries — 'or even the cannibals', he had added — so far as he was concerned. But she had looked at him with horror. 'In the family it is,' she said, 'and in the family it will stay. You treat me right, and I'll treat you right.'

'Nay, lass,' he had said, dryly, 'at the rate we're going on you'll see me out.'

But she hadn't liked what he had said. She had shaken her head and wished he were more like England Bean, a wish which only filled him with horror. And here he was, sitting in the village hall, full to repletion, listening to the growling, unceasing rise and fall of conversation, much of which was about Jochebed. How she would have loved it, he mused.

There was a kind of earnest clattering on the wooden floor as his brother-in-law England rose to make a speech. The noise from scraping chairs and moving tongues alike died. The big man's grey moustache fluffed about his moist lips, and he stood with one hand on his wife's shoulder.

He eulogized his wife's dead cousin, then passed on to his sister-in-law and her husband. 'This has indeed been a good day's work,' he said, 'and there's only one thing been left undone, *as yet*. Over a hundred and fifty pounds has been spent on this funeral — I know, because I've done practically all the ordering — and it's all come out of the deceased's own little fortune.' He smirked at Luke, who felt that he ought to do something in return, so gave two reassuring nods, and went on: 'Yes, there's only one thing to do. And that's to get a really good headstone with what's left.' His eyes shone with malicious satisfaction. 'I feel sure that that is what our Cousin Jochebed would have wished.'

There was a profound silence.

'Well, what do you think?' he asked, turning to Lyddie.

She was sitting at the head of one of the long tables in her brand-new black clothes, a fresh piece of fur dangling from her neck, although the day was sweltering. For the first time for days a smile broke out on her thick, mottled face.

'Please yourself,' she said, in a loud, clear voice which carried to the farthest corner of the hall. 'Please yourself about that. It isn't *my* money. Jochebed left it to you.'

The Mandoline

THE MORNING was still, bright yet ethereal, and an elderly sun had warmed the dead bracken on the hillside so that already it glowed golden brown. For a few days there had been fog and a blanketing silence and drops of moisture hanging stagnant from the leafless twigs, so that now in the sunlight, although it was only November, spring seemed to be poised, motionless but sure, over the far hills.

Two figures were approaching the long, low, stone farmhouse which stood in the middle of the common, one of them wearing nankeen trousers banded against the mud, an earth-coloured jerkin and a newish dark blue cap. He had a broken nose and friendly brown eyes and gesticulated with hands and arms as he walked.

His companion was a very pale, thin youth with an almost expressionless face, his eyes partially enlarged by thick-lensed glasses. His features were small and delicate, his teeth regular but yellowish. He wore the grey-green uniform of a German prisoner, a loose-brimmed cap, the crown of which fitted tightly, and large, heavy boots which seemed to drag along behind him.

The first man, who was a kind of foreman-guard, opened the iron gate of the farmyard, and walking up to the door, knocked in a light, hesitant way. The prisoner stood behind him, looking like some tall, stupid bird. He had not spoken except to say yes or no.

In the low, dark farmhouse kitchen, which opened straight on to the yard, an elderly man and his wife were working, the woman washing cans and the man carefully mending a cracked pipe stem with thin string. They looked an old couple, bent and grey-haired, but neither of them had yet reached sixty years of age. As they heard the low knocking, they turned and went to the door together, being full of curiosity about the two men, one of whom they knew well, the other not at all.

A new road, which ran a lane's-length from the farm, was being built by German prisoners, still retained though the war was long over, and from eight in the morning until dusk there was the sound of continuous noisy activity about the moorland farm, as the grey-green figures broke up the stones which were brought in by lorries from the neighbouring stone quarries. The old people, who were called William and Mary Illingworth, had often seen the prisoners, but had not yet spoken to one of them.

The woman dried her hands and opened the door, looking out past the men into the still autumn morning. The foreman, Sam Proudle, smiled and moved his arms about uncertainly.

'Good morning, Mrs Illingworth. I've come to ask you a favour,' he said, 'but I don't know if you'll grant it.'

'What is it?' asked the woman quickly. In some way, she was afraid. She could not think what a prisoner could require of her, and searched her mind timorously.

'Well, it's a funny request,' went on the foreman slowly, 'I don't know whether I ought to ask you. But I know you've got a mandoline, and this gentleman — ' he waved a couple of fingers at the prisoner — 'wants to know if he can borrow it for one of his kamerads for the camp concert. For Sunday, he wants it, for next Sunday, and a few days to practise in.'

The farmer stood with his hands on the table, looking mildly at the pair.

'Can you play it?' the woman asked the prisoner.

He stood up more straightly, opened his mouth once or twice, and said, 'No, no.'

The foreman explained hurriedly, 'This gentleman plays the piano. It's one of his kamerads that plays the mandoline. VERY GOOD,' he suddenly shouted at the prisoner. He had evidently grown so used to shouting simple English words at the prisoners that for the moment he had forgotten something. In a much lower tone he continued, 'This is our interpreter. I'll leave him with you to explain.' And he went away.

The couple stared dumbly at the tall youth, who looked back at them, his eyes very wide behind his army spectacles.

'Come in,' the woman said suddenly; and to her husband she said: 'He wants to borrow our Godfrey's mandoline.'

The boy stepped over the threshold and stood motionless upon a stone flag of the floor. The old man had retreated behind the kitchen table and remained there without speaking, only looking at the young German with calm eyes. The thin string slowly unwound itself from the pipe in his hand. The woman began bustling about and talking in a high-pitched voice, and outside, in the walled garden which was a continuation of the yard, the sun searched the wet, brown, withered bushes, the dying Michaelmas daisies, and the two heaps of garden refuse beneath the aged pear-tree.

'I have been in hospital,' said the boy suddenly, 'for a long time.'

'Sit down,' said the woman, motioning towards a wooden chair.

He sat abruptly, looking at his muddy boots, the marks from which remained where he had stood. His hands lay lax on his knees. He had not removed his cap. He did not notice the flickering fire, the red grandfather clock in one corner of the room, the two brass candlesticks on the high, narrow mantel-shelf.

'What do you do? In Germany?' the farmer asked in a very loud, careful voice.

'I am a schoolmaster.'

'My son is — was — going to be a teacher.'

'The one who played the mandoline,' the woman broke in. 'Our Godfrey. He played the mandoline.'

The boy looked round, but could not see the mandoline. It was not in the kitchen. He looked towards the farmer.

'Your son?' he asked, searching for words with some difficulty, apologizing, 'I only know English these few months, since I kom heer. Your son, does he not wish to lend the mandoline to my kamerad?'

'My son was killed,' said the farmer harshly. 'In Germany.'

'Oh!' said the prisoner. A pale flush ran slowly over his paler face, and drained away. There was a long silence.

The woman broke it. 'Come into the parlour,' she said. 'We have a piano. Come and play it.'

'The parlour?' asked the boy. He did not understand.

'Come and play the piano,' said the woman, bright-eyed with nervous haste. 'Come with me.'

The boy followed her out of the kitchen, over the flagged hall to a small sitting-room. The sunlight showed crude colour-patches in a faded carpet. Across one corner of the room stood a shiny, walnut-veneered piano, with pleats of green silk showing under an ornamental lattice at the front. The piano was open, and upon the stand lay a cheap copy of some music on which was printed Gem No. 79, Strauss Waltz Medley.

The woman pointed to it. 'Play that,' she said.

The boy peered at the simple music, and sitting down on the piano stool, put his muddy boots on the pedals. His cap was still upon his head.

'It is a long time since I played the piano,' he said.

'Go on. Go on. Play it,' said the farmer who had come through from the kitchen and was now sitting stiffly in a corner, still holding in his hand the half-mended pipe with its dangling string.

There were many pages of music, and the boy played steadily through them. Here and there he struck a false note, and said 'Oh!' in quick shame. The woman had gone back into the kitchen, where she drew down from a high shelf in the cupboard an old coffee-grinding machine. There were a few beans in the brass cup. She ground them, and making one cup of coffee with milk from a jug on the table, took it into the parlour. The boy was still playing.

She put down the coffee on a small table beside him.

'Here,' she said gently, 'drink this.'

At her words, the boy stopped playing in the middle of a bar, and turning, thanked her. The old man had left his chair and could be heard moving in the bedroom above the parlour.

'You will take care of Godfrey's mandoline?' asked the woman anxiously. 'Yes, yes,' answered the boy, drinking his coffee.

'Godfrey played the mandoline. He played the piano, too. We bought the piano for him.' She smiled slightly at her own work-worn hands. 'But now he is dead. The war.' She looked full at the boy.

Again the pale flush broke over his thin face.

After a little while, 'I have had a letter from home,' he said. 'The first in a year. All is well.'

'All is well,' she repeated after him.

'All is well,' he said. And there was again silence until the old man came slowly downstairs, carrying the mandoline in a shiny black case.

He handed the case to the boy, who stood abruptly. Some of the mud on his boots had dried, and fell off in small clumps, silently, as he moved his feet.

'What do they call you?' asked the farmer in the same loud, careful voice he had used before. 'What is your name?'

'My name is Adolf,' said the boy, 'Adolf Klein.'

And for the third time, his face flushed.

'Klein. That, in German, means little, I think.' He smiled, as if it were a joke being called little, who was so tall. But Klein was only a foreign word to the farmer and his wife, and meant nothing.

'Now I shall have to go. They might miss me. Thank you very much for the coffee, and for the piano, and for the mandoline.'

They moved awkwardly to let him pass through to the kitchen and out of the door.

'Come again and play the piano,' said the woman. She touched his sleeve gently, wonderingly, as he crossed the flagged passage again. And as he walked through the house, the boy looked around at everything, at the grandfather clock ticking away the years, at the brass candlesticks polished to a rounded fineness. He seemed to be looking for a picture of Godfrey. But there was no picture, no sign of his death anywhere. Godfrey seemed to be alive in the kitchen, in the parlour, at the piano playing the Strauss Waltz Medley, even carrying the mandoline.

'Yes, come again,' said the old man in his strange, loud voice.

He walked across the yard to the iron gate and opened it, to let the prisoner through, and then looked across the common to the bracken-brown hill, lying drenched in yellow light. His wife joined him, and they stood together in the silence until the tall boy carrying the mandoline was out of sight.